SIT, STAY, MURDER!

A TAMSIN KERNICK ENGLISH COZY MYSTERY

LUCY EMBLEM

This a work of fiction. Names, characters, places, buildings, businesses, products, and incidents are the product of the author's imagination. They bear no relation to actual persons, living or murdered, and every relation to the Malvern Hills, a designated Area of Outstanding Natural Beauty in the heart of England. The place is real, but the characters in this book are not, nor are many of the villages you'll visit.

Copyright © 2023 by Beverley Courtney Ltd

All rights reserved.

No portion of this book may be reproduced in any form without written permission from the publisher or author, except for the use of quotations in a book review.

First Edition 2023

Published by Quilisma Books

CHAPTER ONE

Tamsin sat at the kitchen table with her head in her hands, her eyes crossing, as she tried to make sense of the spreadsheet on the screen in front of her.

"This has to work!" she called out to no-one in particular, running her fingers through her dark hair and making it considerably untidier than it had been. Banjo came trotting over and rested his chin on her thigh, gazing at her with his adoring collie eyes - one blue and one brown - as she found herself absently ruffling his fur.

"We gotta make this work, kiddos," she said, addressing all three dogs, who were now showing an interest as her better tone of voice suggested food or fun may be on the cards.

Hearing the chitchat, Emerald came wafting down the stairs looking the divine creature she was, accompanied by the other divine creature - her longhaired cream-coloured cat, Opal. Emerald wore a long green flowing robe which swirled round her as she walked. With her straight blonde hair cascading down her back behind her, she looked for all the world like a Pre-Raphaelite heroine. She was the sort of person who always made an entrance, as opposed to stumbling into a room as Tamsin felt that she did. She quickly looked down at her scruffy, mud-splattered, trousers and the baggy and rather hairy fleece emblazoned with her logo *Top Dogs,* looked up at Emerald again and sighed loudly.

"What's up honey-bunny?" cooed Emerald in her soft voice. "What's wrong?"

"Oh, it's the figures for the school," said Tamsin, pushing back into her chair, her hands on the table edge, as if she could keep the spreadsheet away from her.

"You know what I'm like with numbers - it's driving me nuts."

"I'm sure it will all work out perfectly - you put so much work into the planning, it's got to work - stands to reason," said Emerald blithely, with the faultiest of logic.

"Well I'll know this week whether this new venture is going to fly, or whether I'm going to be putting myself on the streets in order to pay the mortgage next month."

"If you're going on the streets you may need some different clothes." Emerald raised a perfectly-curved eyebrow at her house-mate. "But this is your new venue, right?"

"Yes," said Tamsin with a pout. "The hall in Nether Trotley. The Great Malvern classes are going fine, but I need more to make this business profitable. If it works out I'll be opening up a whole new area. There's no-one out Trotley direction doing any dog training at all - never mind dog-friendly training like mine."

"Hmmm," Emerald rested her cool hand on Tamsin's shoulder as she leaned over to look at her laptop. "If it works well I may start one of my classes over there too. Is anyone doing yoga there, do you know?"

"I saw a poster advertising chair-dancing for the over-70s - the mind boggles! So it looks as though someone's already doing what you do," giggled Tamsin.

"I *was* going to offer to make you a coffee to cheer you up, but I think I've changed my mind." Emerald tried to affect a snooty look as she headed for the coffee pot, but failed miserably.

"Oh, go on," pleaded Tamsin, "I'm desperate for a coffee - I'll stop winding you up." She smiled as she heard Emerald getting a second mug out of the cupboard, then added, "Actually it could be very good for you.

Nice wooden floor, no smelly carpet. It's very quiet and secluded - middle of nowhere, really. And it's got good parking."

She turned back to her columns of figures, now all starting to swim before her eyes, then slammed her laptop shut. "Let's have that coffee in the garden - it's looking nice out there now - beautiful Spring sunshine."

At the welcome sound of the laptop lid shutting, the dogs all leapt into action and started to twirl around each other, little black-and-tan Moonbeam taking short cuts under the bellies and through the legs of the bigger dogs.

Tamsin loved her work in the centre of rural England - she loved working with the owners to show them a better way of getting what they wanted from their dogs than shouting and yelling at them; she loved being able to sit in her garden to drink coffee in the middle of the day - and what could be better than spending her days with dogs? She had little ambition beyond helping dogs and spending time with them. She had a very strong sense of justice and integrity, and couldn't bear any kind of cruelty to animals - even shouting at them was unacceptable to her!

She carried her coffee out and put it on the arm of the wooden bench, and as she sat, Moonbeam hopped up beside her to play King of the Castle with the other dogs. Emerald decided to sit on the grass, doing a few yoga stretches as she did so. Her serenity was disrupted by shnooffly sniffs and kisses from Quiz and Banjo, who assumed she'd got down to dog level for that very purpose.

"*Ooarrrrch!*" she cried in a muffled voice as she turned away from her two admirers. "It's a wonder to me that you call yourself a dog trainer," she laughed, playfully pushing the larger collie Quiz away, who instantly bounced back, eyes shining.

"The cobbler's children are never shod," replied Tamsin with a smile. She loved that her dogs were so friendly and affectionate to the people they knew. And since moving in, Emerald had grown very fond of them too.

"So tell me about this new class," said Emerald, squinting and shielding her eyes from the low April sun as she looked up at Tamsin, the majesty of the Malvern Hills rising up behind her.

"It was something Sebastian said, actually. One of the few encouraging things he said about my business before he finally shoved off. He pointed out that there was a limit to how many classes a week I could hold in this locality, and that I'd need to branch out to earn more. And of course since he swanned off and left me with all the house expenses, it's become urgent!"

"I do my bit ..."

"I know you do, Emerald - and I'm really happy the timing worked for you so you could move in here."

"It was a piece of luck! When they dropped that bombshell and gave me thirty days' notice I didn't know what I was going to do. Without a car I have to be in walking distance of my classes at Jean-Philippe's."

"Hmm, that's a point - how would you be able to use Nether Trotley then?"

"You know what? Living here has worked out cheaper than where I was before, and with that extra class I was able to fix up at The Cake Stop, I'm actually saving some money. Perhaps I'll be able to get some wheels!"

"And a car to go with them?" Tamsin smiled and, dipping the tip of her finger into the froth on her coffee, looked expectantly at her dogs - who immediately snapped to attention and each offered a trick. Quiz and Banjo did a Sit Pretty, sitting up tall with their front paws dangling, while Moonbeam pushed her bum in the air on the bench beside Tamsin and took a very creditable bow. They were each rewarded with a lick of her milky finger.

"That's terrific! I'm happy for you. And someone at the cafe is bound to know someone who has a decent car they want to sell. Do you know how to drive?"

"It was considered part of my education by my mother, so I learned when I was seventeen. It'll come back ... And yeah, I'll ask Jean-Philippe to ask around when I've amassed enough cash. Not quite yet ... Anyway - tell me more about this new class."

"Well it's not a puppy class this time round. I'm going for a general dog class - any age over six months. So there'll be quite a collection of issues to deal with. And you know me, I love a challenge!"

"How many have booked in?"

"Got six so far - nice number. I'll take another late one if someone shows up."

"And the first one's tomorrow night? Who've you got coming?" Emerald turned herself to face Tamsin and sat cross-legged before her.

Tamsin start counting on her fingers, "There's a really nice family with four young kids and their little dog. Parents probably want to restore some order to the house by at least getting the dog under control. Then there's a woman with a giant breed puppy. Sounded quite straight-laced. Um .. there's another woman with a rescue dog. The shelter say she has to go to classes - it's part of the deal."

"Good idea, I suppose ..."

"I think it rather depends on the classes!" Tamsin grinned. "Then there's a funny old chap who said 'I just wants 'e to come when I calls 'im'. He's bringing cash - 'I don't hold with banks,' he said. Think the dog must have been chasing the neighbours' chickens or something. Then there's a very pseudo-posh sounding woman who has a lapdog - can't remember exactly what right now ... Oh, and Charity has booked in - you know, old Charity Cleveland - isn't that sweet of her? She's a great fan of mine and wants to show solidarity, it being her own local village hall. Of course she does love teaching Muffin things."

"Ah, Charity! What a character she is! I hadn't realised she lived in Nether Trotley. She'll be really useful I'm sure, if you need any help."

"Yeah, always handy to have a friend in the camp! It can be nerve-wracking starting a new class. Some people are far from convinced they've made the right choice when they arrive. They lean back in their chairs with legs outstretched and arms folded. Standard rejection posture! And I have to win them over. Some never get it."

"You can't win 'em all!"

"Do you have that with new people coming to your yoga classes?"

"Yeah, occasionally you get someone who thinks they know it all already, but giving them some hard stuff to do soon brings them back down to earth - sometimes literally! We all develop our tricks for handling students, right?"

Tamsin nodded and smiled knowingly. "Apart from Charity I don't know any of these new students. Should be entertaining! Thanks for the coffee - and for talking me down from the ledge. I'm going to do a bit more on tomorrow's class plans then take this crowd off to the Common for a walk. See ya!"

Tamsin stood up, scooping up the cream-coloured cat from her lap - "How did you get here, Opal?" she said in surprise.

Emerald laughed, "She's been there for ages - did you not notice? Here, give her to me."

Tamsin gently tossed the cat on to Emerald's lap where she immediately folded her legs under her and started purring. Banjo snuffled around her bushy tail prodding her lightly with his nose. The cat spun round and glared at him. Banjo backed off, tail waving gently.

"It's great that they accepted Opal so well," Emerald stroked her cat's ears. "I was worried that there'd be problems."

"I'd be lying if I didn't agree with you!" said Tamsin as she moved towards the house. "But the people who used to live next door had a cat who would wander in here all the time, and they were just fascinated and accepted it, no bother. There was never any trouble, and they're kind dogs, so I wasn't really worried. See ya!" she said again as she stepped back into the house, her clan trotting after her, wondering about this walk she'd mentioned.

How could she have known then how things were about to change?

CHAPTER TWO

Tamsin loved her walks on the Common with her dogs. It was always a bracing walk, as living on the slopes of the Malvern Hills meant that everything was either steep uphill, or steep downhill.

The Hills today looked majestic as they towered above her. It was a beautiful spring day and a fluffy cloud-hat topped the Worcestershire Beacon, the highest point of the spine of ancient hills. The powers that be were planning to upgrade the whole area from an Area of Outstanding Natural Beauty to a National Park, which would give added protection to the landscape Tamsin loved so much.

She loved living in the quirky town of Malvern, with its extraordinary mixture of hippies, scientists in the research facility, and the ordinary townsfolk. It rejoiced in various esoteric events, like the Well-dressing, when all the springs and wells round the hills were decked out in more or less pagan finery and flowers, some real, some paper, and some knitted.

"Hey dogs!" she called, as Quiz and Banjo came bounding out of the hedgerow they'd just been investigating. Hot on their heels came the diminutive Moonbeam - a very small black and tan terrier mix with long thin legs and huge ears, and insatiable curiosity.

Malvern had more than its fair share of strange groups - drumming groups, country dancing groups, magicians, jugglers, artists - always being topped up by the local Art School - dreamers, and poets.

And while the town had the usual chain stores with upmarket and downmarket supermarkets and stores to cater for all echelons of society, it was surrounded by dozens of little villages and hamlets, inhabited by farmers, commuters, townie escapees, and oddball blow-ins. Tamsin knew a lot of these villages well, by virtue of the fact that she did so many home visits to help people with their errant pooches.

"Hey Quiz, whatcha got?" Pausing in her climb to wait for Quiz to catch up after exhaustively sniffing a clump of gorse and young bracken, she looked back over the Severn valley below, across to the city of Worcester beyond the woods to the left, and to the pretty little harbour town of Upton-upon-Severn away to the right.

Reassured the stick Quiz was carrying wasn't a hawthorn, she said cheerily, "You're ok, it's a good stick."

One of the joys of Tamsin's work was to visit people and dogs in their homes for her private training sessions, for those who either needed or simply preferred special attention. So she knew the surrounding countryside well.

She dreamt of having one of those places deep in the countryside with some acres of her own - when she made a lot more money! Perhaps she'd have some goats, which she'd always longed for since being enchanted by some goat kids as a very young child. But Tamsin knew that living closer to the town as she did was the best place for her for now. She'd keep that dream alive, but leave it out there and see what would come.

Just then a mother with young children and a pushchair came round the bend in the path. "This way!" Tamsin called quickly to Moonbeam who had spotted them and was wanting to scamper up to say hello. She was a friendly and harmless little dog, but without Tamsin close by she was apt to get carried away and greet people way too enthusiastically! Moonbeam spun round at the sound of her name and hurtled back to Tamsin's feet for her reward.

"Good girl, here you go," she said as she dished out treats to all three.

"Ok then, time for some fun!" and she pulled her folded-up frisbee from her back pocket and, concentrating on the wrist-flick which produced the floating effect she was after, named the dog she wanted to run for it and whooshed it across the grass at a safe height for them to leap and catch without injuring themselves. She was never happier than when she was out in the fresh air, playing with her dogs - their grace, speed, and agility were an enthralling sight for Tamsin.

Each dog got a turn at racing to catch the toy, snatching it from the air and racing back to her, eyes sparkling.

"Oops!" she said, as one of her throws spun into the ground, while another veered off at an angle and landed in some nettles. "I'll keep practising, doggos, promise."

She smiled at her good fortune, and rehearsed in her mind the appointments she had the next day. The first was in Bingham Parva, to an old lady who couldn't get her frightened dog into the car, then towards Hereford to a house next to the old canal which worked its way through the countryside till it connected with the River Severn - the same river she could just make out glistening in the sunlight down in the valley below her. Then on to a townhouse on a Worcester housing estate before coming home for a break before her new class.

She'd be able to take the dogs with her as the weather was neither too hot nor too cold for them in the van, and planned to find an orchard to walk in on the way back from the canal house. Perhaps the owners would show her a good canalside walk? She'd learnt a lot of the secret walks she loved in this way - it was one of the huge perks of her way of life.

Her happy reverie was interrupted by the sound of small children crying. The family group she'd seen earlier were hurrying down the hill towards her. She told all the dogs to lie down while she stepped forward to help.

"What happened? Did you fall?" she asked the older child as the mother lifted the younger one, blubbing loudly, into his pushchair.

"Nooo," said the child between sobs, "that man ...." and her shoulders shook as the crying took over again.

Tamsin looked about and saw a hunched figure striding up the hill, a small pepper-and-salt rough-haired terrier a few paces behind him.

"It's ok," said the girl's mother, "he's gone now," as she stuffed a dummy into the toddler's mouth which he worked at furiously between tears.

"Whatever happened?" asked Tamsin in alarm. Her lovely Common was being visited by someone who made small children cry? Impossible!

"Jenny wanted to stroke his dog. She said 'Hello doggie' as it came toward her. That's when he shouted at us. Horrid man!"

"What did the dog do?"

"It looked friendly enough at first, but after all the shouting it slunk off behind its nasty owner. Some people shouldn't have dogs!"

"I'd have to agree with you there," said Tamsin. "But hey - would you like to say hello to my dogs, Jenny? They *love* children!"

Jenny stopped sobbing for a moment and her face lit up. "Can I?" she asked.

"Ok, which one would you like to talk to?"

"The lickle one," said Jenny without hesitation.

Tamsin called Moonbeam over and slipped her hand in her harness just in case she decided to jump up to the child. Moonbeam was being an ambassador for dogs, and the little girl didn't need scratches to add to her woes.

The sobs had now given way to happy squeaks and squawks from Jenny, and gurgles from the toddler in his pushchair, reaching out with his arm to touch Moonbeam.

"Jenny's mad about animals, aren't you love?" said the mother, then turning to Tamsin she added quietly, "She'd love a dog, but I've got my hands full at the moment - the thought of housetraining a puppy as well as a toddler is just too much!"

"Well I'm happy to see they've cheered up. I've never seen that man before."

"I hope I never see him again!" said the young mother fervently.

"It's best always to ask before you say hello to a dog," Tamsin said to

Jenny, unable to pass up on the teaching opportunity. "Some dogs aren't mad about children, so just say 'May I pet your dog?'"

Jenny smiled and said in a clear voice, "May I pet your dog?" pointing towards the two collies still lying down.

"Very good! Quiz would love to meet you, but Banjo would rather stay where he is, if that's ok with you." She scooped Moonbeam up under her arm and called Quiz over, who politely allowed a pat from each child in turn before taking herself off back to Banjo's side. A little goes a long way when it comes to strange children, she seemed to be saying.

And after doing their best to restore harmony to the Common, they set off back home so Tamsin could get everything ready for the next day's work, and hopefully, dinner.

CHAPTER THREE

It was a very enjoyable and rewarding morning's work for Tamsin. Having given the old lady in Bingham Parva the help she needed to get her dog - who had been frightened when someone had crashed into her car - to climb happily in and out of the vehicle again, the second visit - to the Canal house - had worked out well. They were a pair of doctors who'd adopted an old labrador from the shelter Tamsin volunteered at, and she remembered gentle Jez well from her sessions there.

The owners were dedicated, kind, and determined to do their best for their old dog, to give him a happy rest-of-his-life. They offered some very good coffee after the session, and Tamsin had time for a chat with them before heading off to the orchard they recommended for a walk. It turned out that the wife was actually a forensic pathologist.

"How on earth did you get into that?" asked Tamsin, aghast.

"Well, the work does have advantages," the doctor smiled. "The patients keep very still and they don't complain!"

"And I suppose they don't call you out in the middle of the night?"

"Actually, they do. Or the police do, on their behalf," smiled Maggie. "Don's a doctor too - so sometimes he's called out to a living patient while I'm called out to a dead one."

Tamsin said her thanks and goodbyes to the new family, fixing a date for her next visit. Don gave a crooked smile as he showed Tamsin to the door. "Maggie's not usually this morbid on first acquaintance. You must accept it as a compliment!"

As she walked to the gate she wondered about the things some people did for a living. "I suppose someone has to do it," she said to her patient dogs who'd been fast asleep in the Top Dogs van. When she thought about it, her own chosen way of life was pretty odd for most people, who were content to put their trust in someone else and work for a weekly wage. Always a bit of a maverick, she'd tried that early on and after a few short months decided it wasn't the life for her! She needed to feel that she was free to dictate her own hours. Money wasn't a driver for her - she just needed enough to live without worry. And that's what was behind her new class.

"Hey doggies! Walk time .." she said as they drove to the place Maggie and Don had recommended. And unloading all the dogs from the back of the van, they set off to explore a new walk in the jigsaw of walking locations that formed part of Tamsin's mind. Gradually the gaps were being filled with ever more fields and footpaths! She knew exactly where she could find a good walk, wherever she went in the Three Counties. And today she was adding a Herefordshire orchard to her mental map.

"I'm going to remember this orchard alright!" she said to Quiz who walked up one row of towering old apple trees beside her, while Banjo and Moonbeam scampered up the next row. There was still some dew on the grass in the shade of the trees, and the dogs' feet were wet and clean. "This is a find. Let's sit on this bank while I eat something."

As she sat to munch her sandwich, and the dogs mooched around sniffing, she reflected on her lot. One of the things she loved about her work was the variety of people she met. She used to think herself shy and awkward - not a people-person at all. And if someone had told her a few years ago that she'd be standing up on her hind legs in front of a roomful of people to teach them, she'd have laughed at the very idea.

But early on she'd discovered that she couldn't reach the dogs she wanted to work with without getting their owners on board first. So, gradually and painfully, she'd acquired some people skills, and found she wasn't as inept as she thought. Just being herself, with the courtesy and manners instilled in her by her firm parents, was enough. Either her clients liked her or they didn't.

But she *always* got on with their dogs! Going through the trial by fire of winning over their owners was worth the effort to get to work with such a huge variety of dogs!

While she'd chosen Border Collies herself so that she could compete in Obedience and Agility competitions, she loved all dogs, and enjoyed the challenge of finding out what made each one tick. Regardless of breed or type, they were all individuals - and so different! It kept her on her toes, finding out the best way to reach the individual dog and engage its mind. A continual puzzle that had to be solved anew each day.

Finishing her sandwich, and tossing some crusty bits to the dogs, she stood up and ruefully felt the seat of her damp trousers, remembering rather too late that it was a bit early in the year for sitting on the grass!

And so her totally satisfying day continued, dog visit after dog visit, dog walk and dog games thrown in. After her next visit, to the young couple in Worcester with their first ever puppy - always a delightful session to do - she got home in time to feed and settle the dogs, grab a snack and her class bags, and set off to Nether Trotley.

She checked she had the hall keys in her pocket - one for the car park and one for the hall - did a quick mental check-over of everything else she'd need, double-checked the student list and her class plans, let out a big sigh and set off - with no little trepidation. Despite all those people-skills she'd acquired down the years, confronting a class of new students was always a challenge.

"But," she reflected, "nerves put you on your mettle. This evening will go perfectly!" she reassured herself, with a prediction that would prove to be very far off the mark.

CHAPTER FOUR

Tamsin arrived at the hall with half an hour in hand. She unlocked the car park, parked her car towards the far end to leave lots of space for everyone else, and headed into the hall.

It was a pleasant enough little place, with heavy curtains either side of the stage, and plenty of dark wood everywhere, which - judging from the smell - the hall caretaker took great pride in polishing. There was a wooden floor as well as wooden panelling to waist-height round the hall. Above the panelling were various disparate items hanging on the walls.

There were paintings from the mother and toddler group who were there in the mornings, alongside fire escape instructions, requests to leave the kitchen clean and tidy, and some old framed pieces of calligraphy commemorating the Nether Trotley dead of two world wars - shockingly long lists for such a small village. There were Alfreds and Ronalds who were privates and gunners, and Tristrams and Reginalds who were officers. There were several Clevelands, she noticed, from the Great War. She must ask Charity if they were her family - such a tragedy to lose all those sons from one home. But she wouldn't be asking her today - she'd save her questions for another time. She shivered at the senseless loss of so many young men, and brought herself back to the matter in hand.

She started to organise her space, setting up a table with a cloth bearing her Top Dogs logo, and all her wares - leads, collars, toys and the like - and arranged pairs of chairs well spaced out in a horseshoe shape. It was essential to keep the new dogs as far away from each other as possible!

And she was still busy getting everything just as she wanted it when the first students showed up.

The door flung open and a large brown dog surged into the room, pulling his owner behind him. She was a mousy-looking woman with a pointy nose, greying hair, grey colouring, a pale grey coat and an anxious expression. She looked as though she were apologising for taking up space.

"Is this the class?" she asked tentatively.

"Sure thing! You're very welcome," said Tamsin, grabbing her list and ticking off a name, clearly identifiable from the large dog. "So you're Susan and this is Frankie?" She bent and offered her hand to the dog, who was very happy to sniff it and encourage a pat.

"Yes. He's very new. I only got him from the dogs' home a few weeks ago."

"That's terrific! You'll love this. Help yourself to a place and settle yourself down," she said, waving an arm towards the half-circle of chairs.

As Susan dithered over whether to sit nearest the door for a quick getaway, or at the furthest point from the table, the door creaked open again and in came a man with three excited boys, bubbling over with childish chatter, and a small white terrier, equally excited. Chas, the father, was in his thirties, and looked very fit and able.

Tamsin welcomed them, noted the children's names and ticked Chas off the list, said hello to Buster, and organised some extra chairs for them. She chatted to the children, encouraging them to tell her about their dog, until the door opened again and in marched a man with hunched shoulders and a little salt-and-pepper dog. Tamsin stifled a gasp as she recognised the nasty man who'd made the children cry on the Common the day before. Chas narrowed his eyes as he watched the newcomer, then busied himself with his children.

Tamsin stepped forward to greet him - she didn't get a chance to greet the dog as the man grumpily yanked him away. So she directed him to sit nearest the door as she turned back to the table, but not before noticing him nod and say 'Evening' to Susan, who blushed and glanced away, fussing with Frankie's lead. "Oh no, why me?" she thought to herself, as she ticked Phil and Scruff off the list. "This man is going to be so difficult!" Then she took a deep breath and thought, "I can only teach him what he'll allow me to - so I can focus on all those who actually want to learn." She couldn't imagine that this man was open to learning - in fact she wondered why he'd signed up to a class at all. "Now now," she caught herself, "don't judge! He's here for a reason ... perhaps he really loves his dog."

By the time class was due to begin, two more students had arrived. There was Charity, bustling and energetic as always - her busyness belying her years, a small person with a round face full of smiles and warmth, and a twinkle in her eye that invited confidences. She greeted Tamsin warmly and asked if there was anything she could do to help. Her little dog Muffin was happy to wiggle about and say hello to Tamsin.

"Gosh Charity, thanks! But I think we're all set - here, have a seat and settle young Muffin beside you."

"She's sadly not so young any more," said Charity.

"We're as young as we feel!" laughed Tamsin.

And Charity, who'd already been to several of Tamsin's classes, pulled a small bathmat out of her bag and laid it on the floor with a flourish. Muffin promptly threw herself on the mat and lay there, tail flipping, looking around at all the other dogs, with bright eyes.

Then in came a round woman who leant heavily on her ornate walking stick as she slowly crossed the floor with a tiny Chihuahua who was anxious to keep out of the way of her feet and the stick. "This is Mr.Twinkletoes," she said imperiously. Tamsin ticked Jean's name with a smile, and greeted the shy little dog as Jean glanced with surprise at Phil, then gave him a peremptory nod as she stumped even more stiffly across to a chair, her face set, nose in the air.

It was about five minutes into the class when the door burst open again, causing Buster to start yapping furiously, and in stumbled a woman with a very, very, large white dog. She struggled to hang onto the dog and her bag, so Tamsin jumped forward to intercept them before the giant dog - a Great Pyrenees - pulled the woman over and caused mayhem in the hall.

"I'm so sorry," gasped Shirley - the last person to be ticked off the list - "I got lost ... these back roads ... I'm so sorry ..."

"That's ok," said Tamsin, "find yourself and Luke a seat. I'll run through what you've missed," and she quickly repeated the housekeeping and safety announcements she'd been making. She noticed the white-faced Shirley stare at Phil before dragging her attention back slowly to listen to her.

Tamsin loved teaching. She loved seeing the look of puzzlement change to a look of comprehension as she demonstrated the exercises with one of their dogs - and especially loved seeing their pride when they saw how quickly their own clever dog learnt and performed.

So she got involved with what she did best. She stopped worrying too much about Phil. She'd asked him a couple of times to stop yanking Scruff's lead, which was wound several times round his clenched fist. And twice he'd said, "I just wants to stop him running off."

"Of course! And we'll be working on that further into the course. But for now I'd just like you to relax the tension on the lead. It'll be more comfortable for both of you." The young boys, clearly used to people doing what they were told, watched intently as the man grunted and yanked the lead again. Tamsin sighed, and turned her focus to those who were doing their best with the exercise.

She had to show the portly Jean how to manage the tiny Mr. Twinkle-toes with her inability to bend down far enough to reach him. Jean clearly adored her little dog and she began to enjoy herself as he responded so well to her - especially when she avoided banging him with her stick.

Shirley was clearly lacking confidence in her ability to control such a large dog as Luke, so Tamsin focussed on teaching her how to manage the lead with ease. And Charity kept everyone amused by taking every opportunity to put Muffs through her paces and do a trick or two. The boys particularly loved this and begged to teach Buster a trick, as they squirmed in their seats, the youngest boy jumping down from his chair in his enthusiasm. They're like puppies, thought Tamsin, never still except when they're asleep!

"Buster will be brilliant at tricks." She handed out sheets of paper and coloured pencils to the children. "We'll definitely be teaching tricks later in the course!" The boys whooped and wriggled in their chairs as she went on, "Here - do a drawing for me, of Buster doing one of Muffin's tricks." They each grabbed some paper and a fistful of crayons and jumped down to lie on the floor to start their drawings.

"I don't hold with tricks," said grumpy Phil predictably. Tamsin chose to ignore this general utterance and continue with her class.

After his dramatic entrance, Luke found his owner Shirley to be so boring that he lay down on his side and slept, snoring loudly.

Tamsin left him in peace while she explained why the type of treats they brought to class were so important, and which ones tended to work best. She had her own stash of wonder-treats, reserving her secret weapon - finely-chopped pepperoni - for the more distracted or resistant dogs. And she chose Luke to demonstrate the power of pepperoni.

Suddenly she had an awake, animated, engaged, dog! So she slipped Shirley a handful of pepperoni with instructions to bring her own supply next week, and watched with pleasure as they started to make progress.

CHAPTER FIVE

In no time at all, it seemed, the class was over.

Most of the students had relaxed and gone with the flow, except for Susan who looked as though she never, ever, relaxed. She had managed to keep Frankie engaged though, with the aid of some of Tamsin's pepperoni - up until she dropped the lot and Frankie scarfed it up in a second.

But on the whole it had been a thumping success! The children had livened it up enormously, and proudly showed their drawings to whoever would admire them (Charity and Jean obliged), and the oldest boy presented his drawing as a gift to Tamsin with a shy smile.

"Thank you, Cameron - I love it!"

She furnished them all with their homework handouts for the week, and gave them a hint at what they'd be doing next week. The boys, having examined everything on offer on the table, insisted on Chas buying a toy for Buster, and both Shirley and Susan chose a better lead for their big dogs.

As they all gathered their things together, Phil had left without a word. Tamsin didn't miss the moment when he pushed past Chas, who gave him a glare.

She sighed. Why was the man so grumpy? He had such a sweet little dog who wouldn't say boo to a goose. She was thinking he didn't deserve Scruff when she caught herself: "Judgy judgy!" she mumbled.

All the others wanted to talk to Tamsin separately, all keen to show how proud they were of their dog, and how clever they were to have landed such a clever companion. It was clear that all the students, bar possibly the one, loved their dogs, and really wanted the best for them. They just needed a little reassurance that yes, they would manage to change the running off, or the pulling on lead, or the thieving - or whatever each one saw as their main problem - without having to resort to strong-arm tactics.

It took Tamsin a while to listen to each one, but she knew it was a valuable time and would pay dividends for the rest of their course once they trusted her.

She was so absorbed that she hadn't noticed the activity around her. As the last person left the hall she saw that Charity hadn't gone - in fact she was busily stacking the chairs while Muffin snuffled about looking for dropped treats.

"Oh Charity, you don't need to do that!" said Tamsin. "And you've packed up my box too!" She hadn't realised that Charity had been busy all the time while she had been fielding questions from the departing students.

"Happy to help - you must be tired after all that. People wouldn't realise how hard it can be to hold a class of people together - you're really good at it! That's why I enjoy your classes so much." She put the last chair on its stack with a crash, and winked as she said confidentially to Tamsin, "As one people-watcher to another, I can see you have a great gift."

Tamsin smiled shyly. She'd had to work hard to develop her way with students, and it was nice to be recognised and valued.

"Well thank you Charity! That's really kind of you to say that. Here - you head home now. You've done most of the clearing up already, so I'll just run around with the broom and lock up. See you at our next class!

And thank you for coming. It was nice to have a friendly face and a bit of support."

Muffin gave Tamsin a last wag as Charity clipped her lead onto her harness again, giving a cheery wave as they left.

As the door closed, Tamsin closed her eyes and enjoyed the silence in the room. Then she heaved a big sigh and whizzed round with the broom. Funny how children can generate sweet wrappers without ever appearing to be eating! And where on earth did those rubber bands come from? Perhaps it's essential kit for the well-prepared 7-year-old. She cast a final eye over the hall - this class was going to be a success, and it was so important to keep in with the hall people, especially the caretaker! They often guarded their domain fiercely, and she didn't want to take any risks.

So, with her box on her hip, she locked the door behind her and made her way to her car. It was long past sunset now, and without the lights from the hall the car park was in total darkness. As she approached her car she saw another car parked beyond it.

"Oh no," she thought. "I have to lock the car park and someone's left their car there! Now what will I do?"

She put down her box as she fished in her pocket for her car key, then jumped in surprise as a little dog crept towards her, tail between its legs, body close to the ground.

"Scruff!" she said, "You gave me a fright!" and the little dog relaxed and came forward to her. So Phil is still here - I wonder why? she thought to herself as she reluctantly peeped round her car to see.

Then stopped dead.

On the ground between the two cars she could make out a dark shape, the size of a man. And nearest to her were two feet.

It *was* a man! She grabbed her phone and fumbled with shaky hands to find the button to switch on the torch.

"No!" she cried, as she bent down beside Phil's head - then recoiled as she saw the nasty wound on the back of his head, and the blood seeping into his collar.

She stepped back, nearly tripping over her box. Get a grip Tamsin! she said to herself. Call an ambulance! But just before she did she went the other side of the inert body and took a look at Phil's face. His eyes stared dully, at nothing.

Tamsin clutched her chest to steady her breathing. She looked wildly about, and listened. Nothing. There seemed to be nobody there. But scared to death now, she grabbed her box and Scruff and bundled them into her car, jumped in and slammed the door.

As her breathing slowed a little, from gasping to something a little more natural, she checked she'd locked her doors before taking her phone and dialling 999.

It took a while to go through the preliminaries before she was able to explain that someone was dead. They asked her to stay right where she was, and not to unlock her door for anyone.

She didn't have more than ten minutes to wait before she heard with relief the wail of sirens cutting through the quiet, dark, night. But in that ten minutes she tried to work out what had happened.

They had all left more or less together, apart from Charity and herself. There had been no noise, no shouts, no barking - nothing. And yet within thirty minutes, somehow Phil had sustained a fatal injury. To the back of his head. How could that possibly be an accident?

She shuddered and checked for the third time that her doors were well and truly locked. Scruff sat on the passenger seat in silence, and she put a hand on his shoulder to reassure him, and herself. She was glad she wasn't completely alone with this horror.

When the police car and ambulance arrived with a blare of noise and a crunching of gravel in the car park she felt some of the tension lift and she started to breathe more easily. "I didn't realise I was so tense!" she said to little Scruff, who had stopped shaking but still looked utterly miserable.

She waited for the uniformed police to jump out and come over to peer at the gap between the two cars, then took a deep breath, carefully unlocked her door and stepped out, leaving Scruff inside.

Suddenly it was all business as the police took over, directed the ambulance crew to check the body and confirm that life was extinct.

"Any idea how long he's been dead," they asked the medics.

"Well I can tell you when he wasn't," said Tamsin. They looked at her coldly and said, "We'll be taking a full statement from you in a moment, Miss. Would you kindly step back and stay right there?"

She decided to keep quiet and leave them to it. They were definitely very formal - didn't they want her help? ... then she thought with a jolt, They think I did it! Noooo! She was a suspect in a violent death ... a horrible crime ... a *murder!*

This was all she needed. One moment her new project was promising to be a success and give her her much-needed boost of income, and now she was caught up in a murder enquiry! And what would happen to her new students? Surely they would all demand refunds if they were in danger of being murdered at class! What about her other students? She could picture them all leaving in droves as she became known as the person whose classes you were unlikely to escape alive!

And it certainly didn't look good for her. She was the only one there. Not another soul. The others had probably parked at the other end of the car park, nearer the hall. She'd deliberately parked at the end to leave plenty of space for them. Why had Phil parked right up beside her car? Had he been meeting someone else?

Her head spun with questions. And a feeling of dread was creeping over her. What had been a great evening, a good start to her new venture, had turned in just a few minutes into a nightmare.

She leant back against the car and waited. And tried to remember the times of events. She knew she'd finished the class at a couple of minutes past the hour, and that with everyone wanting to talk to her, it had been about twenty past by the time they were gone. Then Charity must have left a bit before twenty-five past ... Ah! She remembered when she cast a final eye round the room that she had caught sight of the hall clock, which clearly read twenty-eight minutes past. This meant that Phil was alive straight after class, and ... dead at half past. Now it was quarter to nine: everything had changed so fast.

And it was nearly nine fifteen when the police had finally taken down her statement and organised the removal of the body in the ambulance.

"What do I do about locking the car park?" she asked.

"You can give us that key," the policeman replied. "We'll lock up and secure the car and the car park. It's now a crime scene. SOCO will need to go over the whole place - Scene of Crime Officers," he added, as he saw Tamsin's look of bafflement. "You can go now, but don't go disappearing on us."

"No chance," replied Tamsin curtly, "I have a business to run," and a reputation to patch up, she thought, as she turned back to the car.

"Hang on a minute," said the officer as she put her hand on the door handle. "Did you say this chap was at a dog class? Where's his dog?"

"Oh, he's in my car. I'm happy to mind him till you can find out who the next of kin is."

"We should take him and put him in the station kennel."

"Please don't!" interrupted Tamsin. "He's terrified. He'll be fine with my dogs. Really. And as soon as you've found whoever should have him, I'll happily hand him over. I don't need another dog," she said wryly.

The two policemen looked at each other, and one added another line to his notes as he gave a slight nod. "CID will be in touch with you tomorrow," he said as he clicked his pen, returned it to his pocket, and turned away.

It was with a heavy heart that Tamsin steered her van away from Nether Trotley hall and back towards Pippin Lane and her home in Malvern.

CHAPTER SIX

"I'm damned if this is going to wreck my school!" said Tamsin, as Emerald attempted to soothe her frantic brain by giving her a head massage.

"Just try to keep still, relax those shoulders …" crooned her friend.

Emerald had arrived home shortly after her house-mate, having just been giving a yoga class in the home of one of her students. Without ceremony Tamsin had blurted out, "A man got murdered! My new class is ruined!" Emerald had quickly found a gin bottle and some flat tonic water and fixed a strong drink for her, hunted in the fridge for something they could eat, and generally tried to restore calm.

The dogs were disturbed too, not just from Tamsin's distress, but having to cope with a new dog in amongst them. Fortunately Scruff was a sweet, shy, creature, and was keeping out of their way - moving away as soon as one seemed to want the place he was sitting. She'd already fed the dogs, but not knowing whether Scruff had been fed, she cracked an egg into each of their bowls as a snack, taking Scruff's egg to the next room for him to eat so no-one would get upset.

While she was doing this, Emerald had been busy lighting scented candles and warming her calming essential oils.

"Ok, spill the beans," she said, standing behind Tamsin's chair as her fingers worked the acupressure points on her head.

"Mmm," Tamsin closed her eyes, "that bit was good ... you hit the spot there alright. Well ... " she began, and told the story of the evening's events. By the time she got to, "and then the police let me go," Emerald had finished the massage and was sitting down opposite her with her own much weaker glass of gin and tonic.

"So what are you going to do?"

"I don't know at all. On the one hand I want nothing to do with it - but I can't put my head in the sand! This is going to affect my business - my livelihood. I can't stand by and watch everything I've built up for years crumble away because someone hated this grumpy man enough to kill him."

Emerald folded her long legs up under her on the chair and draped her blonde plait down over her shoulder. "What do the police say? I mean they surely don't actually think you did it? You'd have to be stone mad!"

"I suppose anyone who can wield a hard object and do such a thing to another person must be pretty mad .." Said Tamsin glumly. "To think one of those students in my class is a murderer!"

"But does it have to be one of them? I mean, couldn't someone have just chanced upon the scene and tried to rob this guy? It could be nothing to do with them!"

"It would be nice to think that, but the thing is, the hall is very remote. It's near to the church which is a little way away from the rest of the village. So nobody would be around there. It was dark, and you can't see the car park from the road as there's a big hedge and some of those giant recycling bins in the way. There's just a dilapidated sign - you'd have to know the hall was there."

"Hmm, I see. You did say it was remote."

"And it wasn't a robbery. I saw the police go through the man's pockets and open his wallet which clearly had cash in."

"Ok, tell me who the suspects are. Let's see if we can do a Miss Marple and solve the dastardly crime!"

Tamsin took a swig of her drink, screwed up her face and said accusingly, "What did you put in this?"

Emerald smiled, and stroked Opal who had, as was her custom, infiltrated her lap. "It's medicinal. Drink it."

Tamsin outlined the students briefly for Emerald, beginning with Chas and his boys. "Ever such a nice young man, and the children were very well-mannered, though they're incapable of keeping still. Then there's Susan, grey Susan. Wouldn't say boo to a goose. Jean? Well, between fussing over her tiny dog and hobbling about with her bad leg, I can't see her attacking a big man. Then there's Shirley. Very quiet and withdrawn."

She took another swig of her drink and instantly regretted it. "Charity, of course. With Muffin. And me? No! I want more students paying me, not fewer!"

She put her hand on Quiz's head, which was resting on her lap. "I'm not much use at this. All I can think is I really can't imagine any of them doing it ... Mind you, now I think of it, they all had a bad reaction to Phil when he arrived."

"Really? What did they do?"

"I saw Chas giving him a long look a couple of times. Phil greeted Susan but she was very frosty in return. Jean gave a kind of snort when she saw him. And Shirley looked sideways at him but didn't really react at all. And of course, I told you about the little children on the Common yesterday?"

"The ones who were crying?"

"Yes - it was Phil who'd made them cry!"

"No! He must be a really unpleasant person. Have been, I mean." She paused for a moment, stroking Opal softly. "So you don't think it was any of your students?"

"Can't see it."

"Trouble is, you think that just because they're nice to their dog, that they're above reproach. Didn't Hitler love his dogs?"

"Oh God, don't tell me I have a deranged maniac amongst my students! Someone who sees themselves as a superior being who metes out punishment as they see fit?" Tamsin groaned and took another sip of her drink, grimaced and put it on the table beside her. Looking at the peaceful cat on Emerald's lap, she called Moonbeam - "Here, hop up and cheer me up - you need to earn your keep, you know."

"It seems to me you're going to have to do something. It'll be in the papers tomorrow, and is probably halfway round the grapevine already. Perhaps a visit to The Cake Stop is in order? Enlist Jean-Philippe's help - he'll help put a stop to any gossip."

"That's not a bad idea - I don't have any 1-1s tomorrow, and no classes till Thursday. I can't just sit about here waiting for the detectives to show up. I need to be doing something."

"Tell you what - I'll come with you. I'll show solidarity - and keep my ears open."

CHAPTER SEVEN

So after a night of fitful sleep, Tamsin set off to the coffee shop with Emerald, bringing Quiz along for company - giving her a good run on the way as they took a diversion across the Common.

The busyness, the sounds, the ambience - and Jean-Philippe's friendly face - did a lot to calm Tamsin, as they ordered their usual coffee plus a slice of scrumptious cake to share to cheer them up. Quiz knew where the water bowl was and helped herself to a drink, and enjoyed being greeted by Jean-Philippe - and his trainee barista Kylie who paused to say hello while taking some toasted sandwiches to a customer's table - before she sat patiently beside Tamsin in the hope of a dab of icing.

"*Eh bien*," said Jean-Philippe, perching on the table next to them. "What have you been up to?" he said meaningfully, his bushy black eyebrows raised as high as they would go.

"You've heard, then?"

"It's the talk of the town. When the Three Furies delivered their cakes this morning they were full of it."

"How did *they* know, for heaven's sake?" asked Emerald.

"They're friends of Charity's," explained Tamsin. "They are her disciples - always ready to weigh in when needed."

"So if Damaris, Penelope, and Electra know ... everyone will know soon enough," Jean-Philippe added. "Still, don't worry! We know you're not *une assassine!*"

"Don't even joke about it!" warned Tamsin.

But he went on, "What I was going to say is that clearly it has nothing to do with you. I bet you're worried it'll put people off your school. It'll be a nine-day wonder, *écoutez-moi bien* ... er ... you mark my words!" He beamed with pride, then went on, "The well-dressing's coming up soon, and the procession from well to well will distract them. People will be planning their costumes, getting the donkeys groomed and all the rest. *Oh là là* , the things you English get up to ... it's a *merveille*," he sighed.

"It brings you plenty of business!" said Emerald with a smile.

"*Oui, c'est vrai!* Plenty of visitors all year round in this town."

"Seriously though ... how am I going to get over this? People will leave in droves if they think they're going to be murdered in class! I don't know how long the police will take to solve it. Perhaps it's not high on their priorities ... "

"Perhaps you need to do a bit of sniffing about yourself?" suggested Jean-Philippe. "You know, ask a few questions that the police can't. It's well-known that people tend to clam up if *les flics* ask them things. But they like you. They may open up a bit."

"How can I do that?" Tamsin spread her hands out in question.

"Supposing you drop round to those who were at the hall last night - ask them if they remember anything," Jean-Philippe begin.

"Hey!" Emerald jumped in, having been busy licking the icing off her fingers, "You could ask them where they parked. That's innocent enough."

"Then you can dig in deeper and find out if they knew this dead guy."

"You've got something there - I did kinda get the impression they all knew Phil already, Jean-Philippe. Just little somethings that I noticed. And they were distinctly unhappy about seeing him there ... hmm. I'm going to do that today! If they can help point a finger *away* from me, that will be worth doing!" She took a forkful of cake, "Those Furies may be weird," she said quietly, "but they sure bake a mean cake! And talking of food, I have another mouth to feed meanwhile. Scruff is staying with me - that's Phil's dog," she added for Jean-Philippe's benefit. "I've no idea whether this man had a wife or family … though he was so nasty I somehow doubt it."

She explained about the incident on the Common the day before, and her audience was suitably shocked.

"I don't think we'll be looking to arrest toddlers for his murder," laughed Emerald, "but doesn't that just show that there were probably loads of people who had good reason to hate him?"

"Good reason to hate him doesn't equate to good reason to kill him. There's got to be a lot more to it than that," said Tamsin glumly.

"Unless whoever did it is bats in the bells."

"Bats in the belfry," Emerald corrected Jean-Philippe's English automatically.

"Bats in the belfry, I *see!*" he said gratefully, tapping his head, "creatures flying about in the bell tower!"

"That's it!"

Quiz, who had been dozing beside Tamsin, sat up at this merriment and looked hopefully up at her friend. "Here you go," she obliged, dotting her finger in the crumbs and giving her a lick. Then she emptied her mug of its last delicious contents and put it back on the table with a decisive flourish.

"I think I'll just turn up unannounced at their homes - catch them in and chat to them." She took out her phone and started checking their addresses, and making an itinerary in her notes app. "You free today, Emerald? Want to come?"

"Why not! I may pick up on something you don't," she said eagerly. "And if I'm with you, you can just say we were going somewhere and found ourselves passing them, so thought we'd drop in. Takes the pressure off."

"Sounds like a plan," said Jean-Philippe, standing up and acknowledging Kylie's wave from the counter, where a small queue was forming. "See you later - and don't worry - really. It'll all work out."

"Let's take Quiz home and check for police messages on the home phone, then we can set off. I need to DO something!"

"How long are you going to have to keep Scruff?" asked Emerald, as she gathered herself to leave.

"I guess I need to ask the police that. They said they'd be wanting a statement from me, so I can ask them then. Fortunately," she added, as she pushed open the big door of the cafe, "Moonbeam's taken a fancy to him, so he's not a problem."

So they left the calm bustle and delectable scents of the coffee shop and set off towards the Common again, admiring as ever the huge mass of the Malvern Hills towering over the town and the surrounding villages. What had those ancient hills seen? What stories could they tell?

CHAPTER EIGHT

So they set off together to start their investigation adventure at Charity's house. A frantic yapping greeted them when they banged the heavy door-knocker - which was in the form of the head of a dog with horns. Tamsin and Emerald exchanged glances before breaking into smiles as the door opened and out flew Muffin, delighted to see them both.

"Ooh, come in, won't you?" Charity held the door open wide for them, looking enquiringly at Emerald, who looked for all the world like a slender, graceful, goddess in her close-fitting but stretchy clothes. Just as Tamsin was always dressed for mud, dog hair, and snatching teeth, Emerald was ever ready to adopt an asana or two, even occasionally launching herself up against a wall in a soothing handstand, to the puzzlement of all who didn't know her.

"Thank you, Charity - in you come Muffin - this is Emerald, a friend of mine. We were passing and noticed we were near you. I wanted to have a chat, you see ..."

"And so do I! Such goings-on! Come in my dears - make yourself comfortable." She led them into a small and cluttered sitting room and started scooping cats up off the chairs and draping them over her arm like clothing.

"You don't mind cats do you?" she asked, as she picked up the third, a cross-looking old tabby.

"Love them!" Emerald reached out for a particularly striking long-haired cat in Charity's arms. "May I sit with this one?"

"Oh yes - Sapphire would love that! Oh - and she's another precious stone, like you, dear Emerald!"

"And my cat is called Opal - don't we have a lot in common?" she smiled.

They declined the offer of tea. "We're still full of the Three Furies' cake," said Emerald - before blushing and adding, "Oh, I'm sorry - am I allowed to call them that?"

Charity laughed, "Everyone calls them that, don't worry! Sit yourselves down." She was eager to get started talking. Charity was a small, trim woman who'd never married. Her age was a mystery, disguised by her continual movement and alertness, but she was probably well into her seventies. She loved her home and prided herself on knowing everyone, and their most secret histories. She wore a floral-patterned frock with a hand-knitted cardigan, and her trim cap of grey hair set off the sparkly blue of her eyes nicely.

"Well I always knew that Phil was a bad lot. But I never thought I'd see someone take matters into their own hands like that! Whatever can have pushed someone so far? Such a dreadful thing ... and to think I was right there just before it happened. Or just after, perhaps? Makes me shiver," she added, demonstrating the fact with a vigorous shake of her shoulders.

"That's what I was wondering," said Tamsin. "Well, there's lots of things I'm wondering. First of all, how was he a bad lot? And if you didn't like him, does that mean no-one liked him? Because you seem to like everyone!"

"He was just bad-tempered. Always. I was at junior school with him, so I remember him way back then. Always looking resentful. An unhappy boy with no friends."

"Did he have a bad home life?" asked Emerald above Sapphire's raucous purring.

"Or was he just a few cats short of a colony?" asked Tamsin.

"Bit of each, I think. He was one of those people who had no care about their appearance. Socially inept, I suppose you'd say. His clothes were always basic, and scruffy. Dirty. He had that smell that old men living alone often have. Unkempt. And back in those days, there were no social services to speak of. Things could happen behind closed doors and no-one would be any the wiser. So I think, yes, he probably had a rotten childhood."

There was a silence while they all digested this, and Tamsin asked, "So what did he do that was bad?"

"Nothing major, I don't think. There were little gripes and spats. Who said what to whom, sort of thing. There was a suggestion that he was involved with some missing village cats at one stage, but I don't know if there was any truth in that. People tended to keep out of his way. He was a great complainer. And he made lots of threats - about reporting people for what he thought were slights or misdemeanours."

"So if he's so ... apart ... why do you think he joined my class?"

"That's a bit of a mystery. I think in his way he loved his little dog - oh, where is the dog?"

"Don't worry, I have him. He's safe. Go on, Charity."

".. but he had a strange way of showing it. He was always telling it off. But maybe in private he was nicer. Maybe he thought he should appear masterful when people were watching ... The dog appeared well-fed. Didn't he say he didn't want it to run off? Maybe it had got after some sheep? Or scattered someone's chickens? And maybe that someone had done some threatening of their own. I was puzzled when I saw him there, I have to say."

"But he did actually take part in the class, after a fashion. I didn't know whether I'd ever get through to him, though."

"There were only two things he seemed to care about. His garden and that little dog. Was always with him. And you'd be surprised to see his garden - pretty orderly, when you compare it with his own appearance. And full of veg. He must have eaten well. Of course that's how he earnt his living - gardening for folk."

"I'd like to take a look," mused Tamsin. "And did he live alone? Any relatives? I'm guessing he never married."

"No. Never married. He has a sister, lives over Hereford way. No love lost between them as far as I know."

Emerald paused her cat-stroking for a moment and said, "So there were lots of people he'd managed to annoy over his lifetime?"

"Definitely."

"So who do *you* think did it?" Emerald was ingenuous, and often rather too direct. But Tamsin was glad she'd asked the question - as she wouldn't have quite dared.

"Oh my! I can't imagine any of the others in the class would ever do such a thing."

"But who else could have done it? The hall is pretty remote."

"It beggars belief. I don't like to think of it. I've known most of those people for years."

"You know everyone!" laughed Tamsin. "That's one reason I thought I'd visit you. I bet you know more about them than they do themselves!"

"*You* may not want tea, but if I'm going to relate all these people's histories, *I'm* going to need one. Won't you change your mind?" she got up to move towards the kitchen, causing a flurry of activity in the previously dormant cats. Even Sapphire stopped purring mid-purr and watched intently.

"Go on then, we'll join you!"

They could hear Charity chattering to Muffin and the cats as she prepared the tea.

"This is beginning to feel serious," said Emerald, raising her hands to allow Sapphire - anxious she was missing something - to leap off her lap without shredding her leggings.

"It is."

"But it's ok - it can't be hard. We'll find out what's what, and who's who. Charity's so nice - she'll help us, I'm sure."

"I love that you've jumped on board with this, Emerald! I would feel very lost if I were completely on my own," and the friends exchanged warm smiles, as a huge tea tray came into the room with Charity hidden behind it and animals swirling round her feet.

"Oh here, let me," Tamsin jumped up and took the tray, then wondered where on earth to put it amidst the clutter and ornaments everywhere. Rather than clearing a space on the table, Charity levelled the books and papers and knitting bag and Tamsin nervously lowered the tray there, not letting go till she felt it balance.

"So come on - tell all!" she said as they settled back down, mugs in hand.

"Okay, where to begin? Let's start with Jean, Jean Waterloe. She lives in Baynton - that's a couple of miles in the Gloucester direction from here. She's on her own now. She has a son, Gary, who's in the army I believe. She used to be a tower of strength in the WI - especially the gardening section, arranged all their talks, you know - but since her leg bothers her so much she's cut back on that. She's one of those people who 'enjoys ill health'. She's decided that now she's an invalid she can be looked after, instead of doing the looking after."

"She seemed ok to me? I mean she didn't make a fuss. I had to show her how to handle tiny Mr.Twinkletoes without treading on him or bashing him with her stick, but she seemed keen to make it work."

"I think she likes to play the invalid when it suits her, and when she can get sympathy. She's not *that* disabled. I've seen her run after that little dog when he was a puppy and got out on the road. But I'd think her heart is in the right place. She certainly is fond of her dog. Always a good sign, I think."

Emerald quickly caught Tamsin's eye, no doubt thinking of Hitler again.

"And did she dislike Phil particularly?"

"No more than the rest of us as far as I know. There was the thing about the missing parcels ... but that all blew over. Of course Gary would have been amongst the village boys who used to taunt people, nothing malicious, but he may have annoyed Phil. He's the sort of person young boys would have a go at. But I don't know how much he'd have come into contact with him. Perhaps he did some work over in Baynton?" she frowned as she tried to remember.

"Right. Now, how about Chas and his three little boys? They seemed really nice kids. What about their Mum?"

"I think she's happy to have them off her hands for an hour or so, what with the new baby to look after. If she has any sense she'll have spent the time sleeping!"

"The boys seem to be well brought up, and Chas very caring. How local are they?"

"They're over Lower Thatchall way. They haven't been there that long - just a few years."

"Blow-ins, like me!" laughed Tamsin.

Charity smiled kindly and carried on, "There were just the boys when they arrived. Very involved in campaigning to save Thatchall Infants School. Busy people, you know. They like to get involved. You'll always see them at things like the Well-dressing over in Malvern, the Christmas Lights, and suchlike. I happen to know the older boy, Cameron, goes to the juggling classes over in West Malvern. He's a bit of a scamp and I can just imagine him being a magician or a clown!"

"I've heard about those classes!" said Emerald. "I love that such a quirky thing should have a following here." Sapphire had returned to her lap and her motor was running noisily again.

"Nice boy - he gave me his drawing of Buster," Tamsin recalled. "So what would be their gripe with Phil?"

"I'll have to think about that. Oh! Yes, of course, Phil did some work at Thatchall Infants - maybe they crossed swords there. Chas is on the school board - he was instrumental in saving the school, not just by swelling its ranks by three children when he arrived, but by campaigning hard, approaching MPs and that kind of thing. But Chas has some kind of white-collar job in Worcester. I can't imagine him getting drawn into a feud with a jobbing gardener."

"Susan. Susan and Frankie. She seemed afraid of her own shadow."

"Now Susan's a strange bird. She's lived here in the village for ever - all her life. Her mother was regarded as the local witch. You know, herbal remedies and whatnot. She had a remedy for everything, and they do say that if you got in the family way you could rely on Susan's mother to give you some potion that would remove your problems."

"Golly!" said Tamsin. "A back-street abortionist here in Nether Trotley! Who'd have thought it?"

"Oh, you'd be surprised at what went on. What's always gone on," she added. "Life has never been what it appears to be on the surface. People are the same down the centuries. Only these days people think they've discovered everything anew! The folk used to know - they've always known ... but they had to keep quiet about it."

"Fascinating!" interjected Emerald. "There's nothing new under the sun, my mother used to say."

"And she'd be right." Charity finished her tea, put down her mug on the slightly precarious tray and invited Muffin to jump up into her lap. "Here Muffs!"

"I feel a bit naked with an empty lap," said Tamsin.

"Oh here - grab another cat! There are enough to go round."

"No, it's ok, I'll do. I couldn't stand the interrogation from the dogs when I get home if I arrive smelling of foreign cat! They already think I'm a tart when I come back with strange dog smells and hairs all over me. Anyway, Susan ... she seemed very, um, grey. Grey hair, grey coat, grey face ... Frankie's not grey though."

"Yes. Grey describes her well. She was very intimidated by her mother. Brought up not to say boo to a goose. And she didn't inherit her mother's gifts - or her business nous. Though she does still stock a lot of the more innocuous remedies, and knows how to make them. I wonder if she had a run-in with Phil over a failed remedy?"

"Food for thought. So all that's left is Shirley and her huge dog Luke. Have to say, I love Luke! I wonder what possessed Shirley to choose such a big dog?"

"Maybe she didn't know he'd get so large? I don't know her too well. I've seen her about town a bit - can't miss her, being hauled along by a polar bear! She lives between the Trotleys and West Malvern. One of those funny little houses on its own, with its own acre. She hasn't lived here long - only about seven years."

"Another blow-in, then!" laughed Tamsin.

"Too right," smiled Charity, getting the townie joke at the country-person's expense. "I believe she does something literary - something like that. I remember meeting her in the Post Office once with a big parcel under her arm. She said it had to get to the publisher urgently. That's all I know. I don't know whether she's on her own or has family."

"I do remember her glancing with surprise at Phil when he arrived, but she didn't speak to him as far as I know. Maybe he gardened her acre of land?"

"Maybe so. I can do a bit of asking around if you like. Find out who he's worked for over the last couple of years."

"Good idea. Those are great insights you've given us, Charity! I'm going to talk to all the students anyway - reassure them if I can. I don't want them all to disappear and not show up next week."

"Perhaps you can make sure they all leave together, so no-one's alone in the car park? It's still fairly light when your class starts, but dark enough at the end of it," chipped in Emerald.

"That's a good plan. That should help put their mind at rest. Right, this ain't going to butter me no parsnips! Let's get going." Tamsin jumped up from her chair, causing Sapphire to leap off Emerald's lap, making Emerald squawk and Muffin yap.

"Thanks so much for the tea. If you think of anything else - just let me know. You can always find me at The Cake Stop at some stage of the day!"

And so the two friends left for the next stage of their adventure.

CHAPTER NINE

They chose to start with the next nearest student - which was the enigmatic, grey, Susan.

When they pulled up outside her cottage, they saw that it too was grey and drab, the grey pebble-dash beginning to peel off the walls here and there, revealing rather pleasant uneven old brickwork below. But her garden was startling in its array of colour. One thing she must have inherited from her mother was green fingers. It took a while fruitlessly waiting at the front door before they realised where Susan would be, and started round to the back of the house, where they found an even larger and busier garden, with the back view of a bending figure in amongst the shrubs.

Susan started when they called her. "Sorry to barge in! But we couldn't get an answer at the front door, so guessed you'd be out in your garden. It's really beautiful!"

"Sorry," said Susan, as if trying to disappear. At that moment Frankie bounded down the garden to meet the visitors. Finding one of them to be the source of pepperoni from the class, he was so enthusiastic that his tail whacked Emerald's leg painfully.

Tamsin introduced her friend and explained that they were talking to all the class students to reassure them.

"Let me wash the mud off my hands," said Susan as she led them to the open kitchen door. "Would you like a cup of tea?"

Tamsin exchanged glances with Emerald, wondering how much more liquid they could manage in one day.

"Oh - don't go to any trouble! But a glass of water would be welcome." She wanted to have a reason to stay and talk to Susan a bit.

"This way," said Susan after putting three glasses of water - each with some lemon balm leaves and a tiny sprig of rosemary - on a tray and leading them to the living room. The visitors gazed in wonder at all the pictures on the wall. There were many botanical prints of plants that looked as though they were pages taken from a reference book. And there were photos - old ones, mostly - and some yellowing newspaper cuttings.

"Is this you here?" Emerald pointed to a small sepia photo of a baby in a white frock sitting on a blanket on the ground, smiling up at the unknown photographer.

"Yes, that's me. Don't know why I still have it on the wall ..."

"And this one?" said Tamsin, who'd found a family group featuring what she assumed was Susan at about twelve years old, with a man and a woman.

"Yes that's my mother - and father. He's been gone a long time now. Mum - it was just a few years ago she passed."

"I'm sorry to hear that," murmured Tamsin. "What's this newspaper article?"

"That's when they did a feature on Mum's herbal remedies. How the locals had come to rely on them. The doctor at the time tried to warn people off. All needles and modern drugs he was. No time for the tried and tested medicines. People have used them for generations you know - and without the side effects you get these days from what the doctors give you." She was clearly warming to her subject. "They prescribe one pill. Next thing you know you have to have another to deal with the unwanted effects of the first, then another. There are people I know who are on eight different pills a day! Ridiculous!" she finished with a snort.

This was quite an impassioned speech from the previously diffident Susan.

"So your mother was a herbalist? That's fascinating!" Emerald added with enthusiasm. "I do agree with you, there's far too much reliance on modern drugs. I know they test them and all that, but there are still horror stories from things which slip through the net. Remember thalidomide?"

"A perfect example!"

Seeing Tamsin's puzzled expression, Emerald added, "it caused dreadful birth defects in babies born to women who'd taken it as a sedative during pregnancy. Do you know, my mother was given some once by a friend to help her sleep. But she found her fingers and toes started to tingle so my father took the pills and threw them out!"

"New-fangled things," agreed Susan. "But the herbal remedies have been used for generations. There isn't any danger - as long as the herbalist knows what they're doing, of course! Some of the plants we use would be very dangerous in the wrong doses … very dangerous indeed."

Tamsin decided it was time to move to safer ground, and started to outline her plan for the next class.

"So, there won't be anything to fear - you'll all leave at the same time. It's just me who has to clear up the hall, and I'll leave last."

"But what about you? If there is a madman about, you'll be on your own!" said Susan with alarm.

"That's a point … tell you what - I'll bring Banjo with me. He can do some demos in class, and he's very quick to notice anything wrong. He's a great guard dog! He'll see me safely to my car. And I'll have my phone with me - I checked the signal there when I rang the police, it's fine. Tell me - did you see anything, Susan? When did you leave?"

Susan smoothed out the lap of her dull grey skirt and looked about the room before saying firmly, "I was the first to go."

"And do you know who'd want to kill Phil anyway?" asked Emerald, steering the conversation forward quickly.

"Well he always was a grumpy old so-and-so. A loner. You never knew where he'd pop up. He was always sticking his nose into people's business. Couldn't leave well alone."

"Did he ever poke his nose into *your* business?" asked Tamsin.

"He didn't like my mother. That's true enough. But then he didn't like anyone really. I think he'd had a tough time with his own mother, so perhaps he just didn't like mothers."

"And did he avail of your remedies? He must have got plenty of backache, being a gardener!"

"Oh yes. He would often pop round for a muscle relaxant, or a painkilling potion. They do work, you know!" Susan lifted her chin in an attitude of defiance.

"I'll have to remember that when I next get a niggle," Tamsin attempted to appease her.

"So who do you think did it?" repeated Emerald, "and more to the point - why?"

"It's not for me to point the finger," Susan pursed her thin lips. "But there was someone who was taking a remarkably long time getting her big dog into the back of her car. It puzzled me at the time, but I wanted to get off, so I didn't hang about. Maybe she knows something," she added, with a sly glance towards her visitors.

Once they'd walked back to their car, Tamsin said, "Wow, she was quick to divert any suspicion onto Shirley!"

"I wonder what's going on there?"

"Let's find out! Shirley's next on our itinerary. Hey, this is fun!"

"Ye-e-es, but I don't think it'll be fun when we find out who really did it," Emerald added soberly, as she did up her seatbelt.

CHAPTER TEN

Shirley's house was very different from Susan's quaint old cottage. It was a bungalow from the turn of the century, fairly modern. It had those totally inappropriate curved arches along the front terrace, like a Spanish hacienda, which were so out of place in the Worcestershire countryside, so the building presumably pre-dated the stiffer planning permission guidelines now in place in this designated Area of Outstanding Natural Beauty. They'd never get away with it these days, Tamsin thought. The house could just be seen from the roadway as they turned in a gateway in the very tall hedge and travelled up the long drive. All the property seemed to be at the front of the house, and was largely lawn with a few shrubs near the building.

"I guess they needed a gardener to deal with that massive hedge," said Emerald as they pulled up at the front of the house next to a motorcycle and another car.

"I wonder if she has visitors," Tamsin said, nodding to the vehicles. "Can't imagine Luke riding pillion! She'd never find a helmet to fit him," she laughed. "Let's find out."

Emerald smiled as she rang the bell, hearing the distant electronic chime of Big Ben from inside. "Unreal," she whispered.

It took a while for a young man to appear at the door. "Yes?" he said abruptly.

"Is Shirley in, please?" Tamsin asked.

"I'll get her," he said bluntly, and shut the door again.

"Odd?" Tamsin made a face at Emerald, who nodded.

"Very odd. Wonder who he is," she said quietly, just as the door flew open again and Shirley stood before them, her hand holding the collar of her big Luke.

"Hello Shirley, hello Luke! This is my friend Emerald. We were just passing and I thought I'd drop in and see how you were after all that hoo-hah at Nether Trotley. May we come in?" she added as Shirley hadn't moved.

"Let's go over here." Shirley pointed to a metal and glass table and several ornate metal chairs on the terrace, shut the door behind her and released Luke, who was happy to snuffle Tamsin whom he recognised, and more cautiously Emerald, whom he did not.

They all settled round the table, the chairs being quite remarkably uncomfortable and cold to sit on, and Tamsin began, "I hope you weren't too upset by the news - awful thing to happen!"

"Awful. Yes. But not too surprising."

"Really?" said Emerald, mouth open.

"Well, he wasn't a very nice man."

"But who would actually kill him?" Emerald said quickly.

"How would I know? I left straight away. I saw nothing."

Tamsin logged this mentally, and realised that one of their two visits so far had produced a lie. Which one? How very interesting this was! "Did you know Phil?"

"He did some garden tidying for me a couple of times over the years. And he dealt with that enormous hedge." She nodded to the wall of evergreen between her land and the road. "He was alright at that, though I've no idea whether he actually knew anything about gardening. Not that I do either. It doesn't interest me." She folded her arms and leant back in her chair.

"You have a large place here," said Tamsin, trying to keep the conversation going with the very resistant Shirley.

"I like to have space round me. No interest in gardening. It's a nice open space for Luke," Shirley sniffed.

"So you wouldn't know who'd want to do away with him?" It seemed to be Emerald's place to ask this leading question.

"No. Look, if that's all ..."

Tamsin jumped in and explained her plan about the next lesson, adding. "I'd hate to think you'd be afraid to come to class! I think this way we'll all feel safer. But then you have someone here to look after you! Perhaps he'd like to come, make us all feel better?"

Shirley didn't rise to the bait, and stayed staring back at Tamsin, her lips making a thin line.

"Actually," Tamsin went on, ignoring the silence and feeling bolder, "you're not that far from Nether Trotley. Have you never been that way before? You said you got lost on the back roads."

"No, I didn't say I got lost. I was delayed ... there was a tractor .. er, having trouble backing into a field," she added quickly.

"Oh, that's all right then - my misunderstanding, sorry!"

And as they left this house they both knew they were getting - if not downright lies, at the very least some obfuscation.

"Let's see if Chas can shed some light," said Tamsin as she backed her van to turn out of the drive, at the same time noticing the motor bike again, next to Shirley's car. "I wonder if he'll be home yet."

CHAPTER ELEVEN

They arrived at Chas's home around tea-time - possibly not the best time for a busy mother to deal with them. But the distraction of getting food in front of her excited children was useful to relax her guard.

The house was a modern brick-built one, fairly large, the front garden scattered with an old metal scooter with chipped paint, a small brightly-coloured plastic trike, and three balls - some with tooth punctures. There was a hole and a mass of earth spread about it, with a broken yellow trowel shoved into it. Clearly the children enjoyed plenty of time outdoors.

"Sorry if this is a bad time, Molly! But we were just passing and wanted to catch you in. This is my friend Emerald."

"If you can stand the noise and mess, you're very welcome! Nice to have an adult to talk to," she smiled.

The boys rushed to the door to greet Tamsin, almost dragging her in. Buster was spinning with excitement.

"There's been a MURDER!" shouted Cameron, keen to get the news in ahead of his brothers.

"Yes, a MURDER!" echoed Alex, brother number two.

"Someone DIED!" added Joe, brother three, to make it absolutely clear.

"GUIDE, GUIDE" echoed the baby in Molly's arms, to show solidarity.

"The school is buzzing with it," said their mother, leading them to the kitchen and resuming buttering bread - cutting it up into small fingers to keep her daughter quiet in her high chair while she got the rest of the meal together. "Phil worked at the school, you see, so they all knew him slightly. Though he was never very approachable. Probably just as well in a school …"

"He was *horrible*," Cameron chipped in. "Always growling at us."

"Grr, grr," demonstrated Joe obligingly.

"Where's his dog gone? Did they murder him too?" asked Alex.

"Yes, where's his dog?" the three boys clamoured in unison.

"Boys, boys, boys, let our guests sit down without badgering them." Molly shooed the boys to the table. Two of them sat, but Alex had huge difficulty in keeping still and bounced out of his chair, almost knocking his glass of water over.

"It's ok - Scruff is fine, and I'm looking after him for the moment," smiled Tamsin.

"Phew!" said Cameron, wiping the back of his hand across his brow in a theatrical gesture of relief. But Tamsin could see in his eyes that his concern had been genuine, and she was glad to be able to put his mind at rest over the little dog.

The baby started to wail and point as her bread finger fell to the floor where it was instantly hoovered up and swallowed by the waiting Buster. Molly passed her another piece, "Here you go, Amanda." before turning back to her visitors. "It's an awful thing to happen, however unpleasant the man seemed to be. Honestly, I was surprised to hear that he'd been at the class. I wouldn't have thought he'd like being told what to do by a woman."

"He actually fitted in fairly well - and I think he was beginning to understand what I was showing him. Scruff is a poppet."

"Is Buster a poppet?" asked Joe.

"You tell me! Do you love him?"

"Yes, we love Buster!" Alex jumped off his chair again, saw his mother's face and sat again, almost falling off the side of the chair in the process.

"May I?" asked Emerald, as she picked up another slice of bread to pass to the gesticulating Amanda, who seemed to enjoy squashing the bread in her fists as much as eating it.

"Oh, thank you, yes - keep shovelling it in!" said Molly, as she started dishing up fish fingers and peas for the boys, and mashing some to cool for Amanda.

"I wanted to drop round and reassure you, actually, about next week's class. It's light when class starts but dark when we finish. So I thought that afterwards everyone can go out together, then no-one will be alone in the car park. I'd hate to think anyone wouldn't come because they were worried about that."

"I'll tell Chas. I'm sure he can protect your flock as he herds them to their vehicles!"

"Thank you! That will be brilliant! If there's a nutcase on the loose," she added quietly, "it's best not to tempt fate." But once the hungry boys had their food in front of them they became focussed on eating, so she needn't have worried about upsetting them.

"So what do you think happened?" asked Emerald. "Who could have done this?"

"He wasn't a nice person. Any number of people could have had it in for him. But it's an awful thought, that someone could actually *do* that." Molly cast an eye over her table-ful of children with a concerned expression.

"Isn't it just!" exclaimed Emerald.

"What's your theory? I'm sure you have one," added Tamsin.

"I suppose someone must have known he was going to be there and lay in wait for him. Chas told me who the other students were - I know a couple of them slightly. Hard to imagine any of those women could wield a blunt instrument with enough force to actually lay someone low."

"Have the police been round? To interview Chas?"

"They have - they were round bright and early this morning, just when I was getting the children ready for school. Chas takes them, you know, on his way to work. I'll be glad of the break when the holidays start tomorrow," she sighed.

"And what did they say?" Emerald was agog.

"They just asked Chas what he'd seen. He wasn't able to tell them anything really, as he'd been getting the boys and dog loaded in the car. He left very quickly - he was the first to go, I believe."

"No we weren't, Mummy," piped up Cameron.

"Don't speak with your mouth full," his mother said automatically.

Cameron made a big deal of chewing and swallowing his food, then said, "Someone else went first."

"Who?"

"Dunno. Joe was sticking his elbow into me. I didn't see. But I did hear an engine, driving away."

Molly cast her eyes heavenward as she spooned another mouthful of fish into the baby's gaping mouth, "You wouldn't want to rely too much on these squabbling witnesses!"

Tamsin and Emerald laughed, as Tamsin asked, "When does Chas get back? I'd love to know what he thinks. But don't worry, we'll leave you in peace now - I can see you have your hands full."

"He's got some meeting this evening, so he won't be back for ages anyway. I'll tell him you called." She thought for a moment and said, "Have you spoken to the herbalist one yet?"

"Susan?"

"Yes. I believe there was some bad blood there. But don't mind me," she laughed and picked up the spoon again, scooping some fishy potato mush off the baby's chin.

They got up to leave. "Don't move - we'll find our own way out."

"Oh, Chas enjoyed the class - I meant to say. They're all looking forward to teaching Buster these tricks you mentioned. Haven't heard the end of it."

"They'll love that - and so will I! Great to meet you, bye!"

"Bye!" came a chorus of voices from the table.

"Nice family," said Emerald as they got back into the car. "But not for me ..."

"You aren't going to devote yourself to feeding fish fingers to many mouths?" smiled Tamsin as she put the car in gear and drew away.

"Most definitely not. And I wouldn't fancy keeping house for some male who swans around going to meetings."

"Be fair, he did bring the kids to the class - and he clearly dotes on them."

"I haven't met him, of course ... and I'm wondering why everyone so far has claimed to leave first. Bit of a poser, that."

"That's a very good question. I wonder if Jean will also claim to have left first? Baynton is about ten minutes - and I want to hear more about this Gary of hers. Charity suggested he was a bit of an oik when he was younger."

So they set off on their journeying again, this time to the lady with the bad leg and the stick.

CHAPTER TWELVE

Jean's house was just as Tamsin expected it to be. It was in a row of similar houses, all with bay windows and a gloomy look about them. She had a dark hedge at the front and a small iron gate opening onto a short path to the front door, lined with pink geraniums and a row of taller blue flowers behind them, all standing to attention with military precision. No cottage garden chaos for her!

They stood under the curved brick porch as the doorbell trilled deep inside the house. An answering yip-yip-yip told them that Mr. Twinkletoes was on guard duty. They heard the chain being slid into place before the door opened a crack and a pair of worried eyes looked out at them.

Jean looked quizzically at Emerald with her long blonde hair, then recognised Tamsin and shut the door again, murmuring, "Just a moment." After a pause they heard a tapping on the floor as she returned to slide off the chain. Jean used her stick to keep the tiny dog in the house as she invited them in.

Emerald went into raptures over Mr. Twinkletoes, who seemed just as enraptured with her. Jean smiled as her dog was admired, then led them to the living room.

"What a terrible to-do!" she said, wheezing slightly, as she indicated the sofa for them, and lowered herself heavily into an upright red velvet armchair, her ample hips just squeezing into it. Dressed in a dark red floral-patterned dress it was hard to see where she ended and the armchair began. She propped her walking-stick against the arm and snapped, "Twink, leave our visitor alone!"

"Oh, I love him!" protested Emerald. "Can he sit here with me?"

Jean nodded and smiled fondly again, continuing, "I always knew he was a grumpy old curmudgeon, but I *never* thought someone would do away with him. Imagine! Here in our lovely quiet countryside."

"Awful, yes," agreed Tamsin. "And I wanted to call in to let you know that everything will be alright next Monday, as everyone will leave the hall together, and Chas will be shepherding everyone safely to their cars."

"Oh, that's a relief - I was honestly thinking I wouldn't be able to come again. I'm not quick enough to escape a killer's clutches, you know! And Mr.Twinkletoes did so enjoy the session."

"Did *you*?" asked Emerald quickly.

"I did. Yes! It surprised me. I thought it might be boring - sorry, dear," she turned with a self-deprecating smile to Tamsin, "but I thought you may have us tramping round the hall shouting 'Heel!'"

"I'm happy to say that it's nothing like that! We don't order our loved ones about - we get them to do what we want by much kinder means. You're a mother, I believe - isn't that so?"

"I am. But Gary's long grown and gone. Sometimes I wonder if I was too soft on him ... He's in the army now, you know," she said with pride.

"Ah, I guess you don't see him much then?"

"As a matter of fact he's home on leave now. He's out on his motor bike seeing some friends. I don't know if he'll be back in time for you to meet him," she said, glancing at the dark mahogany mounted clock on the mantelpiece, which ticked mournfully as time passed in this stuffy room.

"That would be nice. Is that him in the photo there?" Emerald nodded to a framed photo on the equally dark mahogany upright piano, of a young man in some kind of regimental dress.

Jean beamed, "That's him! So like his father at that age," she sighed, her expression melting with maternal pride. How different she appeared from the matter-of-fact mother they had just left.

"So tell me, I'm dying to know - who do you think did it?" Emerald leaned forward, the little dog firmly on her lap.

"It's got to be an outsider. Stands to reason. I mean it couldn't have been one of us!"

"But how do you know? Did you leave first?"

"No, I didn't. It takes me a while to get Mr.Twinkletoes fastened in his chair seat and get round to my side and get in: I don't get about as fast as I used to, you know, dear. And something had got twisted in his harness, so it took a while fiddling with it before I could get Twinks safely stowed. By the time I got going, I could see Chas's tail-lights leaving the car park. He's got a big car - to accommodate all those children - so I could see it was him. But, of course, that's not to say he hadn't gone over to talk to Phil. It was dark, and that harness was so fiddly."

Tamsin digested this stab at Chas and wondered why Jean had said that. "Where were the others?"

"I'm sorry, I wasn't paying attention. You don't expect to have to give an account of your movements every minute of the day," she said sharply. "Perhaps they were still inside talking to you? I remember Shirley spending ages deciding on a toy for Luke. Have you asked her why she was delaying going? Perhaps she had a reason …" she sniffed loudly.

"Have you always lived here?" Emerald decided to lead the conversation back to Gary.

"Thirty years now …"

"So Gary is a village boy?" she smiled.

"He is. That's why he still has friends here that he's visiting now. They were content to stay and make their lives hereabouts, but Gary has bigger ambitions," she smiled proudly again. "He wanted to learn a trade and see the world at the same time."

"Isn't it dangerous, being in the army? Doesn't he have to go to all sorts of trouble spots?"

"Catterick Garrison isn't too dangerous," Jean smirked. "But he has been to some difficult places, yes. I think he enjoys danger! He was always chancing his arm as a boy - quite the tearaway," she smiled dotingly, quickly adding, "Of course there was never any harm in him."

"Did *he* know Phil?" Tamsin marvelled at Emerald's ability to ask tricky questions without putting people's backs up. She came over as an eager, inquisitive child.

"Phil's been around for donkey's years." She frowned and looked away thoughtfully. "He did do some work here, now you mention it," she added, as if the idea had only just occurred to her. "Been coming for years, on and off, whenever I needed heavy work doing. So I suppose Gary would have come across him when he was gardening. That's when my leg started being troublesome. I just couldn't manage the garden all by myself any more. Now my leg's got so bad, I haven't a hope. I'm going to have to find someone else ... "

"Your garden has some beautiful flowers!"

"Gardening has always been my passion," Jean said sadly. "I organised all the flower shows for the Gardening Society, and the lectures at the Women's Institute. They could never have managed without me." She smoothed her red skirt over her bulging knees as she preened herself. "I even gave some of the lectures myself, especially as I was one of the most consistent prizewinners at our shows," she lowered her eyes modestly. "And the Gardening Society relied *utterly* on me to organise the competitions. Sadly I had to give up on organising the shows when my leg got bad," she sighed. "I can still manage the flowers. I just needed someone to help out with the digging and suchlike. What with Gary being away, I miss having a man about the place. They have their uses, you know!" Emerald had to look away from Jean's coy expression as she said this, to avoid giggling, so she stroked Mr.Twinkletoes with more vigour.

"So you knew Phil well?" prompted Tamsin.

"I wouldn't say 'knew' as in 'knew well', no. Obviously we didn't move in the same social circles. He was just an odd-job man," she sniffed.

"But you must have got to know him down the years," persisted Emerald.

"He wasn't the sort of person you *knew*. Always kept himself to himself. He had a big chip on his shoulder, felt the world had treated him badly."

"He was right, in the end, so."

And feeling they had fished this pond dry for the time being, the two friends took their leave, once more assuring Jean that she'd be safe and sound at the next class, and to be sure to come.

CHAPTER THIRTEEN

They arrived home to three joyful dogs, one slightly shy Scruff, and an aloof cat. Everything normal here then, thought Tamsin.

She went to the phone, absently picking up her notebook and pen as she prepared to check her messages. She was assiduous about returning calls the same day - bookings were too valuable to miss - especially now when her business seemed to be on a knife-edge.

She'd done what she could with the students directly involved, and she hoped Jean-Philippe was doing his best to stem gossip in The Cake Stop. But there would be plenty of mutterings in the parks and on the Common, where dog-walkers got together to solve the world's problems.

"I'll have to organise something on the Common - perhaps a group walk, to show what a fun school I have," she tossed over her shoulder to Emerald, who had gone straight to the wall to do a handstand and meditate.

"What's that?" she said, as she floated gracefully back to her feet. Tamsin shook her head in wonder. She found being the right way up hard enough, without making life more difficult for herself.

"Damage limitation. Thinking of ways to show people I'm nice and the School is safe."

"Good idea. A group walk would be fun. Can I come?"

"Course you can! And thank you for today - you did the good cop bad cop thing really well."

"I thought it would be better if you didn't ask those questions," she said as Opal, on the worktop as usual, wound herself against her, hinting at food.

The dogs, who had been let out to the garden as soon as they arrived home, came meandering back in. At least Banjo and Moonbeam did, with Scruff trotting in behind them. Quiz had found a sunny spot and was stretched out on the grass.

"I actually would like a coffee now - after all that tea! Can you fix it while I check these messages? There seem to be loads of them ..."

The first three were the usual kind of thing, like 'How can I stop my dog running off?' and the rather blunter 'How much do you charge?' which always puzzled her. Bit like ringing the supermarket and asking 'How much is your food?' Impossible to answer till you know what it is they want! She jotted down the details in her book, planning to ring them all back once she had a coffee in her hand.

The next message was quite different. "Oh!" cried Tamsin, and switched to speakerphone as she waved Emerald over.

I saw what you did. You won't get away with it, the muffled message said.

They looked at each other. "I'm going to delete that straight away - horrid!"

"No!" said Emerald, putting her hand over the phone to stop her. "That's evidence. Or it may be. It's probably a nutcase, but maybe somebody *did* see something. We know it wasn't you they saw."

"You think I should tell the police?"

"I do."

"Ok. I'll save it." Tamsin reluctantly pressed the save button, unhappy to think this nasty message was now still in her phone. It felt too close for comfort.

There was another enquiry about puppy classes - this is something I *can* deal with! she thought - then another surprise call. She flipped to speakerphone again as they both listened. There was a lot of background noise on the message, and the speaker was almost shouting to be heard over it.

'It's Feargal here, Feargal Wallis from the Malvern Mercury. I'm on the 'Murder at the Dog School' case. I'm sure you'd like to get the true story out before the gossip takes over. I'll drop round this evening, see if I can catch you in.'

"Murder at the Dog School?" Tamsin put her hands to her face as her mouth formed a big O. "Journalists! I hadn't thought of them. Should I see him? I don't know what to do …"

"It might be an idea to at least talk to him. Or maybe prepare a statement. You know how they can twist words. Perhaps having him onside would be better than antagonising him so he has to make it all up."

"Don't they make it all up anyway? Oh Lord, this is getting more real by the minute." She went to the next message.

'Miss Kernick? This is Chief Inspector Bob Hawkins. I'd like to talk to you please. Can you drop into the station tomorrow? In the morning if you please. Just ask for me. Er, I know you've already given a statement at the scene, but there are a few loose ends to tie up.'

Tamsin scribbled down his name as she listened to the next and last message - much more the sort of call she expected to get, someone wanting advice about what breed of dog to buy for their household of elderly mother, young children, and plentiful trips abroad. Sounds as if a stuffed dog is what you're wanting, she thought to herself grimly, not a real one.

After working her way through calling back all the dog enquiries, she joined Emerald in the garden again to catch the last of the light. Though it wasn't late, the sun had long dropped behind the towering hills. The dogs flowed out after her, Quiz stopping to sniff Opal who was stretching herself lazily in the evening air, contentedly destroying the condemned plant that she'd chosen to lie on.

"At least I just made a couple of bookings - they're still coming in, so far. Hey, are you in this evening? This journalist fellow …"

"Yep, I'm here. I'm working on a couple of new sequences for flow classes, but I'll just sit quietly in the background and poke you if you are about to say something you shouldn't."

"I suppose it's too much to hope that this Feargal fellow might be nice? Or friendly? Or ethical, even? I don't know if reporters and ethics go well in the same sentence."

"There are some good ones, I believe. They go on a crusade about some injustice. 'The Birmingham Six' type of thing. You'll be 'The Malvern One'," she giggled. "Your master's sure stirred things up," she said to Scruff, who was lying on the grass beside Moonbeam, their paws overlapping.

"You know, Sebastian .. " Emerald raised an inquiring eyebrow. "Sebastian who legged it," filled in Tamsin.

"Ah, him. You usually choose more pithy words to describe him."

"Yes, well. Sebastian always said I should stop thinking small, do something startling, get my name in the papers. I wonder if this is what he had in mind?" She grinned as she stretched her legs out in front of her, her toes stroking the dozing Quiz's shoulder.

"Hardly! But they do say that no publicity is bad publicity. Not sure how true that is when you look at some of the big stories. But I suppose it'll put you firmly on the map."

"I'm not sure it's a map I want to be on ..."

But later on, when there was a knock at the door - there was no doorbell since it drove the dogs bananas, and it was easier to manage them with just a knock at the door - and Tamsin opened it to a thin, tallish young man with red curly hair and a nervous energy about him, she was resigned to her fate already.

"Tamsin Kernick? I'm Feargal - did you get my message?" He started to move purposefully towards her, hand outstretched. She hesitated, then took his hand and stood back to let him in. "Come through to the living room," she said, "I hope you like dogs."

Feargal did like dogs. And the dogs liked him. Very much, it turned out. He had a natural way with them so that even Banjo relaxed and came forward from behind Tamsin to inspect him from a safe distance, neck outstretched to sniff his trouser leg. This, of course, endeared him hugely to Tamsin, and served as a great ice-breaker.

"Thank you," he said, as he found his way to the chair offered and gave a cheery hello to Emerald, who was sitting on the sofa with her legs curled under her.

"Dogs! That's enough now - Bed!" said Tamsin, and Feargal watched in amazement as Quiz, Banjo, and Moonbeam shot to their beds in different parts of the room and lay down. Scruff looked appealingly at Tamsin, who motioned him to hop up on the sofa beside her.

"That's impressive! Do you teach that to your doggy students at your school?"

"They all learn that, yes - but it's not the dogs I teach, in fact, it's their owners."

He laughed, "I suppose they're the ones you have to 'sell'!"

"Yep. They're the ones with the credit cards," she smiled. "But seriously, it's no good me teaching the dog one hour a week if the owners don't know how to do it all the other 167 hours. They're the ones that the dog has to live with."

"That's very true. I hadn't thought of it like that." He got out a notebook and put it down on his lap, unopened. Tamsin looked at it and thought she'd better be careful what she said. "I guess your reputation is very important to you? You must get a lot of business through word of mouth, recommendations from friends and the like?"

"Yes, I do. And I don't know how this is going to affect that. Who'd want to go to a class where you'll be murdered?"

"That's one reason I wanted to talk to you. You can see how I love dogs. I've been reading up a bit about you, and it seems you're one of the good guys - 'all dog-friendly training' you call it on your website? So I thought it would be good to do a little puff-piece about you, perhaps some of your students could say how nice you are, that kind of thing."

"And what do you get out of it?" came the quiet, shrewd question from Emerald.

"All news is good news for me!" He laughed, tossing back his red curls that had flopped forward over his brow, and giving a lingering look at her languid form draped on the sofa. "I'm also covering the murder story. And I can tell you I have a hotline to the police station - I've already picked up some information there. Hawkins has got the case. He's looking towards retirement, and he's only interested in closing cases fast and efficiently. It should all be a nine day wonder. Nobody's that interested in a sour old person getting their come-uppance."

"I'm interested!" Tamsin jumped in. "That was a person! He may have been cross-patchety, but he loved his dog enough to spend his money on bringing him to class. And I won't be able to rest till this is all cleared up and the murderer brought to justice!"

Emerald stared intently at Tamsin, who blushed, shut her mouth and leaned back in her seat again.

Feargal quickly scribbled a note in his book. "Look, have you got any background information I can use in this piece? Like - where are you from, originally? Isn't Kernick a West Country name?"

"I was brought up in the Midlands - my father was reared in Birmingham. His father had come from Cornwall to the Big Smoke to seek his fortune. He was a carpenter by trade, and so was my Dad. My mother was in love with all things Cornish - a real romantic. Hence my first name."

"Tamsin? Is that a Cornish name too?"

"It's the Cornish version of Thomasina. I'm glad she didn't call me that!"

"So what brought you to Malvern, Thomasina?" he winked.

Tamsin glowered at him for a moment. "I was doing some dog-sitting in West Malvern, for an Arctic explorer, would you believe? He was going off on an expedition for a couple of months and wanted his house and dogs cared for. I hadn't long left school and I'd been working in a shop and hated it. I was enraptured at the prospect of spending two months in the countryside. That was how I got here."

"And you stayed enraptured?"

"Doesn't everybody? It's such an amazing place, with all these bits of mini-Malvern villages clustering round the Hills, as if seeking safety clinging to their mother's skirts."

"There are certainly plenty of incomers here, it's true."

"What about you? With your first name and your red hair, you're a blow-in yourself, aren't you?"

"I think my mother was frightened by a leprechaun when she was pregnant!" He laughed. "There's no Irish blood in me - so far as I know. She was never very forthcoming about my father. And yes, I blew in, as you put it, about two years ago, when this post came up on the paper."

"And you stayed? Not gone to Fleet Street? Isn't that where all cub reporters want to be?" asked Emerald, with genuine curiosity.

"I've stayed. Also seduced by the surroundings. Not sure I could live in the city now …"

And so Feargal was accepted into their lives - albeit tentatively - and he got the information he needed for a piece about Tamsin and her school.

"I'll pick up some quotes from students off your social media," he added as he was leaving, amidst the swirl of many tails. "I won't approach them unless they've already spoken publicly, don't worry."

Tamsin closed the door behind him, turned to Emerald and said, "Well, he's a charmer. We'll just have to wait and see what he actually writes."

"Interesting, what he said about having contacts in the police. I wonder if that's true."

"The Mercury comes out tomorrow. We'll just have to see."

CHAPTER FOURTEEN

Tamsin kept her appointment at the Station with Chief Inspector Hawkins. His handle was such a mouthful that she addressed him as Mr.Hawkins, and he didn't seem to mind.

He was efficient but distant. She couldn't get over the idea that she was still a suspect. How could anyone think that?

"Supposing I *had* wanted to murder this man who I didn't know before that evening?" she said, her chin up. "Wouldn't I have chosen somewhere else, and not ruin my school's reputation?"

"That's true enough," conceded the Chief Inspector. "But you'd be surprised how many violent crimes are spur-of-the-moment affairs. This doesn't look particularly complicated or planned. More a spontaneous whack. We are spreading our net though, and questioning everyone in any way connected with the victim."

"Then you'll have talked to the other students, I guess. They all seemed to know him in some way or another."

"How do you know that?" Hawkins asked quickly.

"Oh, I could see a sign of recognition from each of them when he arrived," she extemporised. "None of them spoke to him, but there was clearly something there …"

She didn't like to think she was throwing her own students under the bus, but ... "Do you really think it was one of them?" she asked.

"I can't tell you that, as you well know. But it had to be someone who knew he was there, and bore him a grudge. It wasn't a robbery - nothing was taken."

"And why did people bear him a grudge? He certainly didn't seem to be an attractive man. Not an easy person."

"This is what we will uncover. It'll be pretty straightforward, you mark my words." Tamsin thought of Jean-Philippe trying out that expression in the cafe just a couple of days earlier, and wished she were with him there, and not here in this inhospitable police station with the imposing Chief Inspector. She realised he was speaking again: "It'll be cleared up in no time and you can get back to your dogs."

Tamsin resented his patronising manner, but bit her tongue and kept quiet. She'd been through the whole evening again with him, clarifying timings, and adding in what she remembered of who had left when. He'd made a few notes, but his face had given nothing away. She'd told him also about the nasty phone call to her. He took down the details and said they'd be following that one up. "Like carrion crows round a body ..." he muttered, "All sorts of nasties creep out of the woodwork when something bad like this happens. You could always switch off your answering service?"

"No, no," she said quickly. "I depend on that for my business."

When she described finding the body, she winced at the memory of what had been a person for so many years laid low in the dust of the car park. "Someone must have really had it in for him, to hit him so hard."

"It seems it was a fortuitous blow, and caught him on an old injury. It wasn't that hard - just chance that it hit that spot."

Hmm, Tamsin thought to herself. That means it could have been one of the women, not just Chas.

So she had plenty to think about as she walked to The Cake Stop to see Jean-Philippe, and enjoy feeling safe and secure again.

"I think I'll have a Flat White today, please," she said to Kylie who was manning the counter.

"Coming up!" she twittered, not forgetting to add, "And anything to eat?"

"Just the coffee today - gotta watch that waistline!"

"You look great - it's all that gadding about in the fresh air with dogs that does it," laughed the trainee barista who today was wearing her uniform shirt over the shortest of short hot pink ra-ra skirts, showing off a pair of very shapely legs that - Tamsin reflected grumpily - seldom walked anywhere.

She took her steaming coffee to an armchair by the window, and was soon joined by Jean-Philippe.

"*Eh bien,* all good?" he asked.

"Delicious! And I have to say Kylie's coming on, isn't she. She's becoming quite an asset."

Jean-Philippe leaned a little closer and said, "I wondered what I'd done when she first arrived! The pink spiky hair could have put people off. But in fact she's turning into quite a draw. She's popular. *Sympathique.* And she brings us up to date!" He leant back in his chair and raised a gallic eyebrow, "You are naked today. You have no dog?"

"I've just come from the Police Station. A Chief Inspector Hawkins - have you come across him?"

"*Non.* Not a customer. And not an opener of church fetes, or switcher-on of Christmas lights, as far as I know ..."

"He seemed alright. Bit brusque, but I suppose he's not meant to be friendly. Apparently he's nearing retirement and wants a clean sheet, so he's aiming to clear it up quickly. I can only hope. I've been to speak to all the students at that class to reassure them." She enjoyed another sip of her Flat White. "And I'm planning a big dog walk on the Common - I'll get as many past students as possible to join in. That should show a bit of solidarity. I see a lot of them there and on the Hills anyway."

"Let me know when it is, and I'll make sure to mention it to all the people who come in with dogs!"

"You're a brick, Jean-Philippe!"

"*Une brique?* I am part of a house?"

"Exactly! You're solid - dependable. You support everyone."

"I have learnt another of your strange expressions ..."

Tamsin smiled back at her friend. "So have you heard any gossip?"

"Not gossip exactly, but I've heard a few mentions. And I've always jumped in and said they don't need to worry, that you have a great school and you don't murder people. Often. Only people who are nasty to their dogs."

"Well thanks, Jean-Philippe," Tamsin grinned.

"Oh, and there was this," he added, getting up and fetching a paper from the rack. "Have you seen it?"

Tamsin had already managed to forget that today was the day the Malvern Mercury came out, and grabbed it hungrily.

"I'll leave you to read it - but it seems to be friendly, on the whole," he added as he went to assist Kylie with the sudden influx of walkers who had formed a queue, with their knapsacks and their walking poles threatening to knock everything over every time they turned to talk to each other.

Tamsin eagerly found the page with the article - 'Local dog school soldiers on despite fatality".'Things obviously moved quickly with modern newspaper technology. Feargal must have written the article late last night - or perhaps he'd had most of it written already, she wondered to herself. How could he have got those quotes from students so quickly? Crafty fellow!

But it became clear as she read that some of it was a re-hash from previous articles in the archives. And yes, on the whole it was supportive alright.

She was not mad about being described as "reassuringly capable", or "not your usual bossy dog-lady" with a "mop of windblown hair" (she really must get to the hairdressers soon) and "a comfortable dog-friendly appearance", though as she looked down at her scruffy jeans and Top Dogs hoodie she thought that was probably fair enough. But she was happier with appearing to be massively popular with her students, and reading the nice comments about how she had changed people's lives with their dogs. As that was her overall aim, that came over well.

The photo he'd fished out of the Mercury Photo Library was from a family event she'd held the previous year, with her beaming in the sunshine surrounded by smiling children and their dogs. Happy days! That's the sort of photo she'd like from the walk she was planning. She could get Emerald to take loads - perhaps Feargal may be interested?

By now most of the walkers had settled and Jean-Philippe had drawn several tables together for them - which were now covered in cups and mugs and plates full of toasted sandwiches and cake. Tamsin averted her gaze from the walnut cake which seemed to be popular with them, and a touch on her arm startled her.

"Charity!" she said, as she saw who it was. "Good to see you and Muffin," and she leant to offer her hand to the little dog to sniff. "Want to join us?"

"I was passing and saw you in the window," she said. "Not stopping, but I will take the weight off my feet," and she sat down in the other armchair with a sigh, dropping her carrier bags beside her feet for Muffin to inspect with her nose.

"You make me sound like a lady of ill repute," laughed Tamsin.

"Bless you. Thought I'd just drop in and say hello - make sure you're keeping chirpy. I saw Damaris this morning. They're full of it!"

"Did the Three Furies know Phil? Silly question - they know everyone."

"Yes, they knew him, and they had some very interesting things to say ..." Charity leant forward confidentially, "Apparently there was bad blood between his mother and Susan's mother - the witch as she used to be known. I wonder if her potion didn't work, and that's why we had Phil?"

"Goodness! That would certainly be a reason for enmity. And I suppose if Phil knew, it would make him very resentful of the witch - that had her potion worked, he wouldn't have been born. But that's only the workings of your mind, isn't it, Charity? Nothing to base it on?"

"Well, she was much in demand in the bad old days, before it was easy to prevent unwanted bambinos. And no, I've no evidence for that. But it's the sort of thing that could persist. Phil had a way of making snide remarks, and who knows but he said something about her that got back to

Susan's ears? A-a-and," she said eagerly, her eyes sparkling, "another thing: I happen to know that young Gary had a run-in with Phil. Damaris saw them in town when she was delivering. He'd made some disparaging remarks about why Gary had to run away and join up. Suggestions of some sort of foul play in the village. Maybe he was shooting his mouth off to Jean, and endangering the fond view she has of her son?"

"You're full of imagination, Charity. You should write books."

"You're not used to how these things go in a village. Families' fortunes rise and fall - 'From corduroys to corduroys in three generations' - know that saying?"

"They better themselves then drop back to their previous social status?"

"That's right. There's history. And feelings that go back generations. They don't forget ..."

"I'm blissfully unaware of that. Where I grew up people came and went all the time. And it's easy to be anonymous in a city. I suppose everyone sees your dirty linen, year in year out, when you live for ever cheek by jowl with your neighbours?"

"Too right. Oh, and Electra said something that piqued my curiosity too. She said she'd seen an argument between Chas's wife and Phil at the school. They do sandwiches for the school too, did you know?"

"No, I had no idea. That's quite a cottage industry they have going. Molly never mentioned an argument when I dropped round there yesterday. Curious ... Perhaps I'll drop in on the Furies. Do you think they'd mind?"

"They'd *love* to see you!" said Charity, happy to encourage this new connection.

"Oh, and if they do a lot of this catering .. I'm planning a walk on the Common - just to get some good publicity for the school. Perhaps I should make a family outing of it and provide some refreshments?"

"You could get people to chip in - you don't want to have to pay for all that yourself, surely? Could get expensive."

"Hmm. Perhaps a very small contribution. I can carry most of it, if it's a form of advertising. My accountant would be impressed!"

"Evening's probably the best time to catch them. They're up to their elbows in flour and packaging the rest of the day."

"They're entrepreneurs, like me," laughed Tamsin. "I'll look forward to visiting them - and I won't be able to resist their walnut cake if they offer it!"

"All in the line of duty," smiled Charity, gathering up her bags and with an effort pushing herself up on her thin arms from the depths of the armchair. "Come Fluffymuff!" she called loudly to her dog, causing several of the walkers to look round in surprise, then giggle and point when they saw she was talking to her dog who had been scavenging under the tables.

She has no idea, Tamsin smiled to herself as Muffin trotted happily back to her owner to have her lead put on, and she gave them both a cheery wave as they left the cafe. She wondered for a moment if she should have told Charity what the Inspector had said about the strength needed to despatch Phil, then reflected that it was probably best to keep it to herself. Charity was after all the Malvern bush telegraph - the Malvern Clarion to compete with the Malvern Mercury!

"No peace for the wicked," she said to Jean-Philippe as he looked over from chatting to the walkers, "I'm off to plan my walk! Thanks for the paper," she added, as she tucked it back in the rack, folded so that her article was showing.

She set off on the walk home, via a shop so she could buy her own copy of the Malvern Mercury.

CHAPTER FIFTEEN

Emerald insisted on coming along to meet the Three Furies. They were a legend in the town, and she couldn't resist. And they both had a sneaking wish that they'd be offered cake! Emerald, thought Tamsin, was one of those annoying people who could enjoy huge slices of cake and still look like a wraith.

So they set off together in the early evening so Emerald could get back for her class at Jean-Philippe's after the visit.

The house was on the eastern side of the Malvern Hills, up a steep road. So its front garden was in shadow most of the day, and looked damp and Victorian, all privet hedge and mossy grass. The house itself was a stone house looking every bit its nineteenth-century origins. They pulled the rope which caused the old bell to clang.

It was Electra who opened the heavy wooden door. She looked vaguely at them, no spark of recognition - or anything else much - in her eyes.

"Hello," said Tamsin brightly, "I'm Tamsin - Charity suggested I drop round to visit."

"Ah, Charity," nodded Electra, opening the door wide and bowing slightly as they entered. She took them into a sitting room that looked unchanged from the last century. Heavy dark brown velvet curtain blocked a lot of what little light was trying to seep through the window. It was like something from a horror film, dark and foreboding and cluttered to the ceiling with knick-knacks and books. Tamsin jumped as from behind her came a whirring sound followed by a creaky 'cuckoo, cuckoo, cuckoo …' as an ancient cuckoo clock, resplendent with carved leaves and roof, announced the hour.

They looked around them like children in a crammed antique shop. Things glittered amongst the gloom, and curious masks and fabrics hung on the small patches of wall not covered with bookcases and glass cabinets containing trinkets and strange objects. What paintwork they could see was dark brown - a colour popular about fifty years ago, probably the last time the house was decorated. It was like a mad museum, thought Tamsin.

But for all that, the welcome was warm. Penelope, buxom and large, commanded them to sit as they repeated that they were friends of Charity's.

"Any friend of Charity's is a friend of ours," said Penelope, leaning back in her armchair.

"And we love your baking!" added Emerald, tossing her long hair over her shoulder. "We always look forward to visiting The Cake Stop to sample your latest creation."

The three sisters smiled and nodded to each other.

"I wondered," said Tamsin. "I'm planning a big dog walk of all my past students. So they can support my school and - and show I'm not a murderess! Would you be able to supply some sandwiches, or rock buns or … what would you suggest? It'll be in the open. If it's raining we'll just have to turn my van into a food truck!"

They fell to discussing this idea animatedly, each sister contributing some thoughts. They were like a trio of birds, all chirruping excitedly.

"Ok, I'll get you more details in a couple of days - numbers, quantities, that kind of thing. Thank you!" said Tamsin. "I hadn't realised you did sandwiches as well, until Charity mentioned that you supply the school."

"We make a lot of things, for a lot of places," Electra sounded mysterious - as seemed customary for her.

"There's that school, and the cottage hospital takes some. Also the Town Hall when they have a function. Businessmen's clubs, breakfast clubs - all that kind of thing," said Penelope with pride.

"Would you like to see where we make them?" Damaris was perched excitedly on the edge of her chair. In contrast to the booming voice of her sister, she was small and childlike, in her voice and her manner.

"We'd love to!"

And here was yet another surprise. In contrast to the old-fashioned living quarters, the cluttered living room and the equally gloomy hallway, with artefacts and pictures covering the brown walls between dado and picture rail - a fair amount of dust accumulating on them - their kitchen was sleek and streamlined and sparkling, a mirage of shiny stainless steel.

As they entered the room, Damaris switched on the bright fluorescent lighting, and an extractor fan hummed into action.

"We have to comply with all sorts of regulations just to turn an honest penny," Penelope explained with her stentorious voice, looking at their open-mouthed expressions.

"But we don't have to change the rest of our house at all," squeaked Damaris.

"They can't change our home!" Electra added to the chorus, providing the tenor line.

Tamsin and Emerald admired the industrial equipment, the huge fridges, ovens, and sleek stainless steel surfaces. While the sisters clearly loved chaos, this room was pristine. The empty work surfaces gleamed, the twin sinks were empty, even the taps were polished.

"I have health and safety regulations I have to abide by," said Tamsin, "but nothing like this! You must have a booming business?"

"People always want to eat," said Penelope.

"And we love to make lovely food," added Damaris.

"We make good food," said Electra.

"Good food," all three chorused.

"Let us adjourn to the salon while Electra prepares some tea for you,"

Penelope swept before them, back down the brown corridor to the brown room, where she turned on a few dim lights which had found a patch of empty surface to rest on.

"So you're the one who found the murdered man," piped up Damaris, excitedly.

"I'm afraid so. Horrid experience," Tamsin shuddered.

"He had it coming, you know," Penelope boomed. "He was always poking his nose in where he shouldn't. You never knew what he was going to come up with. He was the sort of person who'd notice something, then spin a web round it. Crafty. Then he'd let you know that he'd seen something. People didn't like him."

"But he was indispensable," chipped in Damaris. "Everyone used him in their gardens at some time. He used to keep our privet hedge in order. Awful things - grow all over the place if you don't keep them in their place."

"So who do you think killed him?" It was Emerald who came out with this question, in her usual innocent fashion.

"It could be any number of people who had reason to resent him. I understand you had a few of them at your class, Tamsin."

"You don't think they joined the class on purpose in order to .. to murder Phil?"

"It's possible. Some people have dark minds."

"I find it hard to believe any of them did it. Perhaps someone sneaked in to the car park and lay in wait for him under cover of darkness?"

"I can believe anything of that particular collection of people," said Electra as she trundled in a trolley laden with tea-things, and most of a splendid cake, decorated with smooth white icing with a silver design on the top. "You mustn't be deceived by appearances, you know."

"Charity seemed to think you knew something about them .."

"If you mean Susan, then her mother had a lot to answer for, if you ask me," said Damaris, passing a cup of tea and a slice of cake to Emerald.

"With her potions, you mean?"

"Back in the day, before doctors were all-powerful, it was up to people to find their own cures," Penelope explained. "There was no health service then. Everyone would have gone to the likes of Susan for remedies. Naturally some of them would have backfired - had unwanted consequences."

"Or wanted ones," added Electra mysteriously.

"You mean her one-stop abortion clinic?"

"A lot of people would want to have kept that quiet. And if you can get rid of babies with a herbal concoction, why not tiresome husbands?"

Tamsin gasped. Who had she been entertaining in her class! "Right ... but why would Susan want to kill Phil?"

"He had a real down on her, because of her mother. Susan carries on the business in a small way, but confines herself to run-of-the-mill cures, for headaches, sore feet, that kind of thing." This from Penelope.

"And she has an excellent cream for burns - I've used that on a number of occasions when I've been rushing in the kitchen and scalded myself," added Damaris.

"So Phil didn't subscribe to these medicines?" Tamsin asked her.

"He thought that Susan's mother had tried to do away with him. Before he was born. He had a seething resentment of her. And remember, he lived alone most of his life. Not sure how close to reality he stayed." Electra poured more tea into Tamsin's cup.

"He thought his mother had tried to abort him with one of Susan's potions?" Emerald was open-mouthed. "That would certainly explain his attitude to her ..."

After a pause while they digested this, along with another mouthful of delicious cake, Tamsin said, "And what about Gary, Jean's son? Was there some disagreement there?"

"Oh yes, that had been simmering for a long time," Penelope helped herself to another large slice of cake, as the cuckoo popped out again with a ping and its creaky voice to announce the half hour, making Tamsin jump. "Gary was always a bit of a tearaway, running around with the Blakes and that type - well-known ne'er-do-wells, the Blakes. It seems Phil knew enough about their shenanigans - not-so-funny tricks and japes - to suggest that he'd have to sign up for the army to avoid prison."

"There was a brawl outside The Boot one night," Damaris cocked her head questioningly at Emerald, indicating the last of the cake. Emerald patted her tummy and shook her head with a smile. "Wild words were said, but they all ran off before the police arrived."

"Gary's on leave now," murmured Tamsin. "And one of the children said they heard a motor that night. Maybe it was a motorbike, not a car they heard. I guess coshing people on the head would be easy for a soldier to do."

"His mother is so protective of him. Great big lummock of a man. But she dotes on him. Won't hear a word against him."

"I kinda got that impression too," said Tamsin thoughtfully.

"And where does Chas fit into all this?" prompted Emerald.

"Ah now - Chas." Penelope folded her arms across her ample bosom. "He's ambitious. Wants the perfect life for his perfect family. I think anyone who threatened that would be in trouble."

"And what would threaten it? His family seem nice enough - nice house."

"Perhaps if someone suggested that Amanda was not his?"

"Is she not?"

"Who can say? But people can suggest things. And that would not be good if you were poking a bear by saying something bad about their cub."

"Chas looks in total control - but maybe he was pushed beyond endurance?" suggested Electra.

"Oh my goodness!" Tamsin felt exasperated. "The more I learn the less I understand. And yet .. someone did this awful thing, and my school will stay tainted till they can find out who."

"*They* may never find out. If they don't know which questions to ask. That Shirley knows more than she lets on, that's for sure," said Damaris, tossing another suspect into the mix.

"I think I'm going to have to sleep on all this. See if something pops into my mind - some connection that makes sense of it all." Tamsin and Emerald rose, and thanked the three sisters effusively.

"Thank you for showing us your lovely kitchen," said Tamsin as she clasped one sister's hand after another. "The cakes will taste even better now!"

And as Emerald took Electra's hand she paused and said quietly, "You see things, don't you, Electra."

Electra cast her eyes down and nodded slowly.

"Has anything come to you about all this?"

"She'll tell us when she's good and ready," butted in Damaris. "It's a gift. She has to wait for it," and she put her hand on her sister's arm, as they all processed to the front door, and the Three Furies stood watching as Tamsin and Emerald left.

"That's a bit left-field," said Tamsin. "What was all that about?"

"I just had a feeling," said Emerald mysteriously. "Seems I was right."

"Then I wish Electra would have a vision or revelation or whatever it is, and see whodunit - and soon!"

As the two friends walked back down the steep road towards home, they passed the church noticeboard, which sported one of Tamsin's flyers for her training. Two women were studying the notices.

"Top Dogs. You don't want to go there - you'll get your head bashed in," said one, pointing to Tamsin's poster.

"Is it true then, what they say?" said the other, eagerly.

"About the cow that runs it? Yes, apparently the man was rude to her in class and she went out and topped him."

"Well I never. I thought she was meant to like people. Maybe she only likes dogs."

"Awful temper she has, they say ..."

Tamsin's jaw dropped. This had to stop! Emerald grabbed her elbow and pulled her past.

"Don't mind them. They're just gossips. Nothing better to do. It'll all pass."

"It won't pass till we've nailed this .. this .. " Tamsin stifled a sob, and Emerald slotted her arm into hers.

"Come on. Time for some dog therapy for you - and I have to collect my gear and head off to class."

CHAPTER SIXTEEN

This is the best way to think, said Tamsin to herself as she breathed in the fresh morning air (there was always plenty of that at the top of the Malvern Hills!) and trudged onward and upward, her three dogs enjoying the freedom of the vast open spaces, and Scruff kept firmly on a lead. She didn't know his proclivity for running off, and that was the last thing she needed - especially now the sheep were out on the Hills.

Her own dogs were fine with sheep, due to her careful early training that mutton was not on the menu, and they totally ignored them. She was always on the lookout for something spooking the sheep and setting them running though, as sheep stampeding was a sure way to get a dog's interest! Sheep actually teach dogs to chase them, she thought, as she walked past a large flock peacefully grazing.

And Phil had taught people to dislike him - enough for one of them to have reached the end of their tether and take a pop at him. Though that's not to say only nasty people get murdered. It only needed the other person to snap. And that was it. Deed done.

After all the talk yesterday, the thinking she wanted to do on this walk was the planning of her Publicity Walk, as she was naming it to herself. Trouble was, those other thoughts kept impinging. It was hard to get them out of her mind. Really the police seemed to be doing very little. Perhaps Chief Inspector Hawkins was hoping his retirement would arrive before it got solved, so he could shovel it off to his successor. And what she'd gleaned so far about the possible suspects wasn't making much sense to her.

She turned it all round and round in her head. One of her new students - or someone associated with them - seemed to have to be the murderer. It was really hard to comprehend. She tended to attract kind and thoughtful people to join her school, not nutcases or criminals! But Emerald was right when she alluded to Hitler. People can still love their companion dog and have a warped sense of right and wrong.

Perhaps if they felt beleaguered, that they had nowhere to turn ... pushed beyond their ability to think straight ... perhaps that could send them over the edge - into the darkness of killing.

And other darknesses were attracted to this too. She thought of the nasty phone message threatening her, suggesting that someone had seen her in the act of murdering Phil. "I suppose the police can find out where the call came from," she said to Scruff, who was trotting along with her quite nicely, his initial inclination to tow her along on the lead having lessened as they climbed.

"And I wonder if anyone else got the same message? Hey Moonbeam, what do you think?" Moonbeam had come over to join the conversation, to see if there was anything in it for her.

"And if so ... I wonder if they've reported it." It would presumably rule out that person. Oh no! she thought, they could be just saying they'd had an anonymous call in order to get themselves ruled out. Wheels within wheels.

All the fingers seemed to be pointing to Susan at the moment. But there were also dark suggestions about Jean's Gary and Shirley's mystery man.

Tamsin reached the top of the Worcestershire Beacon, and sighed with pleasure as she looked out across the wonderful green landscape to the spread of counties visible from that height. On a clear day you could actually see thirteen of them! But Tamsin could only pick out the nearest on this cool and misty day. The Beacons were a chain of bonfires that would be lighted to send news across the country fast - a mediaeval SMS system. And they were always placed on the highest point. The next nearest was Herefordshire Beacon, which she could see down the spine of the Hills, the peak surrounded by its ancient fortifications and earthworks. And so the news - of an approaching army, perhaps - would travel all the way down the country, into Wales, down to Land's End.

And more recently, during the last war, she had heard, people would be posted on the beacons to spot fires quickly from their high vantage point. Presumably they had one of those wind-up field telephones to report their sightings? How things changed!

She had formulated her plans for her Publicity Walk by now. She'd ensure that every single past pupil of hers would be invited somehow or another. She'd see if Feargal could get something into the Mercury for her. Providing the refreshments should bring more folk. She'd have to try and assess numbers in advance so she could order the food - she was working out in her mind how she could get people to RSVP - perhaps a voucher towards some classes would encourage them to put their hand up?

She also decided on the date - a Sunday would be best. But ten days was too long to wait! The evenings were getting longer, so it could be next Wednesday. That would give her time to contact everyone by email, newspaper, word of mouth, or pigeon. And most of her past students were people who would be home by 6, and it was early enough to bring the children, who'd still be on their Easter holidays.

She set off down the Hill again with four weary dogs. Her three had wrapped up their adventuring for now and were happy to trot along beside or behind her (though Moonbeam always had to be out in front).

She took a last look at the magnificent view as she made her descent, the further hills fading into the mist, the Welsh Black Mountains completely hidden from view, a warm sunset glow bathing the scene with apricot in the gaps between the mist.

Back home, the dogs all peacefully snoozing (three of them had walked at least three times the distance she had!) she set to work designing a flyer, and crafting an email invitation to send to her whole School. If only one in ten of her past pupils turned up, she'd have a huge gathering. It would be great fun! She had a few "trusties" she could space out along the length of the crocodile to make sure everything went ok. And there would be a pause in one of the big open spaces on the Common for some fun and games.

She'd park her van with all the food in at the best place in the car park. She'd be leaving Banjo at home for this - he really would not enjoy having to confront so many strangers and dogs. But it would be a nice outing for Scruff, so she'd take him.

And she felt lighter of heart than she had done for several days. She always felt better when she was cooking up ideas, planning things, looking out for a new direction, and as a cloud had landed on the Trotley enterprise for the time being, she could focus her energies on the Publicity Walk.

And thinking of who on earth could have "dun-it". Would they show up at the walk? And were they thinking of killing again? There was no escaping that thought.

CHAPTER SEVENTEEN

Next morning Tamsin took her USB pen to the print shop to get her flyers printed. And as it was conveniently just up the hill from The Cake Stop she dropped in there. Everything in Malvern was either 'up the hill' or 'down the hill'. Living on the side of a mountain certainly kept her fit! She was feeling positive and proactive: she'd already spent an hour that morning emailing all her students to invite them.

After her long walk up the Hills the day before she persuaded herself with little difficulty that a slice of the Furies' famous walnut cake was in order. So she sat down in the window armchair with a large coffee and similarly generous helping of cake before her. Today she'd brought Scruff with her for the outing. Did some people actually move about this earth without a dog by their side? She found the thought disturbing, and dismissed it to start in on the cake.

She was relishing her first blissful mouthful when Jean-Philippe came over to join her. The cafe was quietish at the moment, and Kylie was well able to manage the intermittent flow of customers.

"*Eh bien,* how's it going?"

"Ah, Jean-Philippe. It's so nice to see a friend. I'm feeling a little beleaguered, to be honest."

"And who is this?" he asked, nodding towards Scruff.

"This is Scruff. The Victim's Dog," she said, as Scruff happily moved forward to sniff Jean-Philippe's outstretched hand.

"And a key witness ..."

"Do you know, I'd never thought of that! Of course he is. Perhaps we just need to organise an identity parade and Scruff can finger the culprit?"

"Not a bad idea. Seriously. And why are you feeling beleaguered?"

"Gossip. People think I did it because I'm just a nasty person who has a pathological dislike of the human race."

"Hmm. Don't think that quite describes you. I'd say *'difficile'* rather than 'nasty'." Jean-Philippe gave a wry smile, and flinched as Tamsin feinted a face-slap.

"But I'm fighting back," this through a mouthful of cake.

Jean-Philippe raised a thick black eyebrow.

"I'm organising a big walk you see, so dog-owners can show solidarity with me. At least, it's going to be a big walk, and anyone who turns up will of necessity be a supporter."

"That sounds like a good idea. How are you going to publicise it?"

"I've just ordered hundreds of flyers to leave everywhere - you'll take some, won't you?" She paused for his nod, then continued, "I've already invited all my past students personally - there's over a thousand of them! It's amazing how they add up over the years. I bet you can't count the number of customers you've had in that time! And the Three Furies are doing the catering. We'll turn my van into a food truck for the day."

"Have you thought of getting it into the local rag?"

"Yes! I've met one of their keener reporters, and I'm going to ask him if he'll feature it."

"Would that be Feargal, by any chance?"

"It would! Know him?"

"Who don't I know?" he winked. "Feargal comes in here from time to time, when he's working locally. Seems a good egg - isn't that what you say?"

"If you like reading Bertie Wooster, "a good egg" is perfect! But I'm not sure if Kylie would have any idea what it meant."

"I know reporters are right down there on the popularity scale, along with debt-collectors and politicians, but he seems to be pretty straight."

"So far you appear to be right. I do hope so, as he has my future in his hands. He could say awful things ... But he seems to genuinely like dogs. I'm going to give him a ring this afternoon. Emerald will be there on the day, and she'll take some photos for me for my social media pages, but it would be great if we could have an official photographer. Images of me surrounded by laughing children and bouncing dogs, sort of thing; huge mass of people and dogs spreading over the Common."

"That would be helpful, I would think. When's it all happening?"

"Wednesday. Short notice, I know, but I don't want to wait too long. I know some people will welcome the opportunity to show solidarity. Look at this ..." she tapped on her phone to find her email. "Wow! A load more responses! And," she scrolled through quickly, "they're all Yeses, and looking forward to it! That's a relief."

Jean-Philippe smiled encouragingly at her as he got up to help Kylie with the queue which had suddenly lengthened with four mothers with pushchairs. "Bring those flyers in when you have them. I'll do what I can. And - according to what I overheard yesterday - you may want to take a closer look at Phil's house."

"Oh? Who was this? Why?"

"I didn't recognise him. A youngish man. He was telling his companion that the secret lay in the house. Maybe he was talking nonsense ..."

"Who was his companion? Did you recognise them?"

"Nope. Another young man. All you English people look the same," he winked as he straightened the chair. "But he was wearing motorcycle leathers," he added as he left.

Tamsin frowned and turned her full attention on her cake, giving the patient Scruff a crumb or two - but not for long, as the door opened and in came Shirley. Scruff turned and let out a peal of sharp woofs at her.

"Scruff! Hush! Here have some more cake ..." she tried to calm him, as Shirley looked towards her with a frozen expression, glancing with horror at the dog, before turning on her heel and leaving the cafe.

A little later, as she finished her coffee, having long since cleaned her plate of every last delicious walnutty crumb, Jean-Philippe wandered over to her. "Who was that? Maybe the key witness is telling us something?"

"Oh Lord. That was Shirley. She was there that night. Her first class."

"And why would she have bumped off her classmate?"

"Well, she's very stand-offish. Distant. He did do some garden tidying for her. But I don't know how often. It was like getting blood out of a stone, trying to get information from her. I don't even know if she'll show up next week."

"So why do you think his dog kicked off like that?"

"It could be complete coincidence - she did look a bit stiff and furtive. But I don't know ... maybe he's going to be upset with all the people he saw that night. You know what, I'd already planned on bringing him to the walk, so perhaps ... "

"I wonder if I'll be able to get there and see this? I don't think I will - I'll have to check the roster. But I do think it's worth watching out for."

As Jean-Philippe returned to the counter, she noticed the four mothers were all staring at her, while one of them whispered to the others. Tamsin stood up and straightened her jacket, gathered up Scruff's lead and stared right back at them with a friendly smile plastered over her face. They all looked away and started chatting artificially to each other.

"Come on, Scruff," she sighed, "Let's see if by any miracle that printing is done - it would save us a journey."

And she headed off up the hill to the shop.

CHAPTER EIGHTEEN

Tamsin was thoroughly examined by nose by her three dogs when she got back, and they were pleased enough to see their new friend Scruff too, who quickly joined Moonbeam for a chase and frolic in the garden while Tamsin started making a list of all the places she could leave leaflets.

She was full to the brim with cake, so there was no need to make lunch, though "There's always a need for coffee!" she said to Quiz as she filled the kettle then called up the stairs to see if Emerald was in.

She heard a door open and then a soft dot-dot-dot down the stairs as Opal made her way down, pausing halfway to stretch mightily and yawn. She was followed by Emerald moving languorously.

"What news from the battlefront?"

"Well," Tamsin filled the mugs. "Jean-Philippe reckons Feargal is '*un bon oeuf*'," she laughed, "and someone thinks that Phil's cottage holds the secret."

"Sounds very Boys' Own." Emerald smiled her thanks as she took her mug.

"And I've got a stack of flyers for the Publicity Walk! The thing that's going to bolster my reputation. I've already had loads of Yeses from students - I'm so relieved. I'm going to ring Feargal and ask him to cover it - before and during. You still up for taking some photos for me?"

"Sure - of course! I'll be able to watch our suspects amongst all the others, always assuming they come?"

"Perhaps the culprit will feel it's important to show up and look normal."

"Or claim a headache and lie low .."

"Well I'm going to put this out of my mind for a moment and sort these flyers. I've got a couple of home visits this afternoon, so I'll be able to drop them all over the place on my travels. I've got time to ring Feargal and the Furies first. Gonna do that now. See ya!"

So while Emerald went out with Opal to join the dogs in the garden - except for Banjo who always liked to keep close to his person - Tamsin picked up the phone and began with Feargal, fondling Banjo's ears all the while.

"Tamsin!" he answered promptly. "News?"

"Yes! I have a plan .." and she outlined the Publicity Walk for him.

"Sure I'll come. I'll get Jeff to come too - he's one of our photographers. I'd like to take a look at these suspects. Want me to put something in about it in advance?"

"Well it's too late for the weekly edition, isn't it?"

"Yes, but the online version is updated daily. I'll put something in - use a nice photo of you and some dogs. Have you got anything suitable?"

"Plenty of photos, yes."

"Just buzz one over to me today. And any other news?"

"Something odd happened. I was in The Cake Stop - you know Jean-Philippe I gather - and Shirley, one of those students, came in. I had Scruff with me and he barked like mad at her. She looked aghast - thunderous - then turned on her heel and left. What do you make of that?"

"Very interesting. Do you think Scruff's going to solve the murder for us?"

"That's just in films. Poor thing is altogether rattled. That's why I took him with me, to enjoy a bit of normal life. I know he went everywhere with Phil. And there's something else too .." She told him what Jean-Philippe had picked up about the cottage.

"Now we can do a bit of real sleuthing!" responded Feargal with glee. "When do you finish today?"

"I'll be back here around 7."

"Let's head over a bit later and take a look at this cottage. Who knows what we may find under cover of darkness."

"You want to break in?" Tamsin sounded scandalised.

"Mmm, just a bit of creative investigation."

"I'm not going to get arrested for housebreaking as well as murder!"

"Don't worry. We'll just have a bit of a snoop. Should have gone there already. There've been photos of the Village Hall in the report in the paper, but not his house."

The meeting time fixed, Tamsin got on to the Furies next.

"Hello?" said a querulous voice, "Dodds and Co?" It sounded as if Damaris were unsure and asking the caller!

"Hi again Damaris! It's Tamsin. Thank you so much for showing us round your kitchen and giving us that sumptuous tea! I've got an update for you on that order."

"Ooh, I'll just put you on to Penelope. Just a moment ..."

After listening to her footsteps leaving the phone, then heavier footsteps marking the arrival of the senior Dodds sister, Tamsin told Penelope about her projected numbers. "I think you'd better make these sandwiches bitesize! And nothing difficult that people can't eat - like peanut butter or fish."

With more decisions made, she rang off and sighed. "It's worth a few bob to invest in restoring my reputation, Banjo Bunny. I'll view it as an advertising expense. This had better be as good an idea as I hope." She turned to look straight at Banjo, "Or else it's bread and pull-it for us!"

And so the afternoon passed with two very engaging home visits - to a young couple with a brand new puppy who was keeping them up all night, and an old lady who'd adopted an 8-year-old dog who spent its time trying to tunnel out - and she managed to offload a couple of hundred of her flyers to various shops and restaurants along the way. Her own vet took a big wodge, promising to display them on the front of the counter, and the groomers were happy to take a handful.

A bunch here and a dozen there, got her through a good number of them.

"I'll have to spend tomorrow and Monday dishing out the rest of them," she said to her empty van. "They're no use sitting in my house! And all this extra walking means I can have another slice of cake next time I go for coffee," she chuckled in anticipation.

She'd set out without any dogs as they'd have had to spend too long in the van while she worked, and she missed having someone to chat to. So she was reduced to talking to herself, albeit a bit shamefacedly.

"Now for Phil's place," she muttered as she checked her phone.

Feargal had arranged to meet her on the way to Nether Trotley so they were less conspicuous. They drove in his anonymous-looking car the rest of the way, then stopped short of the house and walked the rest of the way in the gathering dusk.

Phil's front garden was neat and tidy - a closely-clipped hedge either side of the garden gate, a gravel path to the front door, and lawn either side. The grass was already sprouting daisies, and there were little green seedlings poking up in the path.

"How quickly it returns to the wild," she said quietly to Feargal, who was craning his neck to see the front door.

"That door is open," he whispered. "Stay here," and he eased the gate open as quietly as he could, walking on the grass to avoid crunching the gravel.

"Hey - don't leave me here!" Tamsin whispered hoarsely and bounded after him, being careful to walk on the grass too.

Feargal used the back of his hand to ease the door ajar. At that moment there was a scurrying noise as someone rushed to the back door at the other side of the house, and ran out, slamming it behind them.

"Hoy!" shouted Feargal, racing round the side of the house. Tamsin stayed frozen to the spot, breathing heavily.

But in a few moments Feargal was back again. "You alright?" he said, looking at her ashen face.

She nodded, "Did you see who it was?"

"No. Too dark, and they were in a dark hoodie. But they moved fairly quickly. Don't think it can have been one of your older students."

"Maybe it was just some ne'er-do-well taking advantage of the empty house."

"Or maybe it was someone looking for something? Let's go and see."

"Shouldn't we call the police?"

"After we've had a shufti," he said, tapping the side of his nose. "Don't touch anything. Just keep close behind me. We'll make sure there's no-one else here."

Tamsin, her heart in her mouth, followed right behind him - clutching on to his shirt-tail as they entered the dark house - and glancing nervously over her shoulder as they went In.

The inside of Phil's cottage was as dull as the outside, but not as neat. There were some gardening magazines and an empty mug on the low table in the living room, next to a sofa, one end of which was coated with Scruff's hair along with a paper with notes made on the runners and riders for a race meeting. The room was nondescript - soulless, the paintwork dark and grimy, the furniture looking as though it had all been there, unchanged, for at least seventy years. On the hearth a blackened brass coal bucket glowed in the gloom. Unlike some of the other houses she'd visited this week, the place was pretty bare, no ornaments or pictures. Just the basic necessities.

The kitchen sported a cooker with a stained and dirty hob under the used frying pan, an old electric kettle which had never been cleaned, and a plate with congealed egg in the sink, along with the eggshells and some burnt toast crumbs.

"That's what he must have had for supper before the class, egg on toast," Tamsin said sadly. "It's all so wrong!"

There were some clothes hanging on a clothes-drier - one of Phil's check shirts, a pair of greyish underpants and a few odd socks. In the growing darkness they could see a kitchen cupboard was pulled open, and some packets of sugar and tea lay spilt on the floor.

"Depressing," said Feargal.

"Here's Scruff's bed," Tamsin pointed to a heap of hair-covered blankets under the little table. "He did care. A bit."

"I'm going to check upstairs." And so saying, Feargal climbed up the steep stairs, keeping to the edge of the treads.

"He's done this before," thought Tamsin as she stood still in the middle of the kitchen, wondering how soon they could get out.

"Nothing," Feargal spoke in a normal voice as he returned to the kitchen. "No sign of disturbance up there. Let's see what they were looking for in the cupboard here."

He shone the light from his phone into the back of the cupboard. "I can see some bills slotted between tins of dog food. And here, what's this?" He reached into his pocket and pulled out a pair of latex gloves.

"I don't believe this," hissed Tamsin, still reeling from the whole experience.

Feargal slid his gloved hand behind the tins and drew out a small medicine bottle. An old-fashioned dark brown, ridged bottled with a cork. They peered at the label. "It's all smeared - can't read it," said Tamsin.

"But it looks hand-written." He pulled the cork and sniffed at the contents. "Smells minty."

"All I know from detective stories is that cyanide smells of almonds," said Tamsin. "What are you expecting to find?"

"No idea. But this probably came from Susan."

"She did tell us he was one of her customers. And if she was going to do him in, poisoning him would be the easiest way."

Feargal put the bottle back where he'd found it. He shone the torchlight around the kitchen. "I don't think we're going to learn much more here. Best tell the police, I suppose. You didn't touch anything?"

"Nothing."

"Sure?"

"I've kept my hands in my pockets from when you told me not to touch anything."

"Good for you! Let's go." And they went out through the front door, Feargal hooking his gloved finger behind it to draw it almost closed, as they'd found it. Then pocketing his gloves they headed back to his car.

Tamsin was still shaking when they arrived back at their rendezvous point. "Here, I'll follow you home," offered Feargal. "I don't think you're cut out for this!"

"Give me a snarling, slavering, ferocious dog any day!" she said with feeling. "That I can manage, no trouble. Creeping about dead people's houses - no thanks." She got into her driving seat, wound down the window and said, "Yes please. Do follow me back - just to the end of Pippin Lane. I'll be fine once I'm on my own road. And here - take these for your announcement," and she handed him a couple of flyers. "I know you and your twitchy nose. You're going to follow this up aren't you?"

"Yes, and it's easier if it's me who tells the police. They expect me to be snooping about. I'll just tell them the door appears to be open and the property needs securing. Then my informant in the station will be able to fill me in on what they learn," he grinned. "Come on, let's get you home. I think you need some soothing canine company."

CHAPTER NINETEEN

Tamsin was glad that she gave herself Sundays off. She spent the morning listening to music - a bit of Vivaldi always brightened her mood - and doing some housework, before setting off with the dogs to a quiet and little-known nature trail in the Severn Valley. Today she could look up at the majesty of the Malverns as opposed to surveying the valley below from the top of them.

She enjoyed the beginnings of the flowering hedgerows - Wood Avens, Comfrey, Cow Parsley - all dancing in the breeze and scenting the air. There was apple blossom just showing on the gnarled and twisted old apple trees in the now-abandoned orchard the path went through. It was grazed by sheep later in the year, who enjoyed the windfalls while fattening up for the winter. These fields would soon be a blaze of yellow once the buttercups filled them - then she'd laugh at the dogs with their yellow muzzles and chests. At least the buttercup dust brushed off them easily, unlike the knots of burrs and cleavers they'd pick up in the late summer. Untangling Quiz and Banjo's trousers and tails could take her hours, so her visits to this trail were carefully scheduled according to the season!

Once the dogs had run themselves to a standstill - with Scruff having had a chance to join in, safe enough in this secluded place far from the road - they settled happily in the van to snooze while she set off to deliver more flyers.

Dropping into the little food shop in Middle Trotley, she collided with Susan, drab and grey as ever, rushing out through the door.

"Ah Susan, just the person!" Tamsin took a flyer from her stack and handed it to her.

Susan looked suspiciously at her. "What's this?"

"Did you not see my email? It's a walk I've planned to celebrate Spring. It'll be fun! See there," she pointed to the flyer in Susan's hand, "there'll be games for the dogs, and food. Frankie will love it!" she added, seeing Susan's doubtful expression.

"Would it be good for Frankie?" she gazed up at Tamsin.

"Yes, he's a friendly dog, and he'll enjoy meeting the others. You may too ..."

"If Frankie will like it, I'd better come. Do I need to bring anything?"

"That's great! No, just yourself and your dog - a water bottle for yourself if you'd like. The dogs will drink from the stream. And you can join us in the car park if you'd like some sandwiches after."

Susan nodded and turned to go.

"Will I see you both tonight?"

She nodded again, opened her mouth to say something, but closed it again firmly.

Tamsin came back via Baynton, so she wasn't surprised when she found Jean in the garden centre there with her little dog standing between her and a friend. She was leaning heavily on her stick until a favoured plant at the back of the display caught her eye and she waved the stick to point it out to her companion.

"Hello Jean! Thought I might see you amongst the flowers!" she called gaily as she approached her.

"Oh hello my dear." She turned to her companion, "This is Tamsin. She teaches the class Mr.Twinkletoes is attending."

"You mean .. ?" began her companion, till a prod with the stick on her toe silenced her.

"The police have been round *again*. They're trying to break down my alibi!" Jean simpered. "But I can only repeat what I told them - and you - the first time. I saw Chas leaving before me, but didn't notice anyone else. What's this?" she asked, nodding at the armful of leaflets Tamsin was holding.

"Oh, this is for the walk on Wednesday - did you see my email? It's going to be such fun - Mr.Twinkletoes will love it. Lots of people to admire him!"

"Ah yes, I did see that. You're assembling all the suspects together!" she giggled. "I'll just join you for the end of the walk if that's alright with you. Can't go far with my leg."

"Whatever you can manage will be great. And - 'the suspects' as you put it, will all be assembling this evening, no?"

"Of course. That was my little joke. Yes, I'll be there tonight. Twinks loved his lesson, you know. I'm going to pick up some more of that sausage in a moment." She beamed as she took her companion's elbow and steered her away.

After leaving a stack of flyers with the friendly girl at the checkout, Tamsin realised she had just enough time to go back via Lower Thatchall.

As she approached Chas's house, she saw a car had just stopped outside and the driver was emerging from it. It was Shirley. And once again Shirley decided that discretion was the better part of valour. As she caught sight of Tamsin pulling up behind her, she leapt back into the driver's seat and sped away, her tyres spinning.

Goodness, she really doesn't want to talk to me! Or .. perhaps she didn't want to be seen here at Chas's house?

She saw two of the boys staring eagerly out of the window at the activity in the road, then the front door slowly opened to reveal Cameron, arm stretched up to reach the Yale lock, with his sidekick Joe behind him.

"Hello you two!" she said as she crunched up the path.

"Who is it?" called a distant voice from inside.

"It's ok," called Tamsin over the boys' heads, "I'm not stopping. I just wanted to get these leaflets about the dog walk to as many children as possible and, of course, they're on their Easter break this week ... So I thought you might know what I could do. Perhaps there's a playground, or adventure place they go to?" she asked Molly as she joined them in the hall, wiping her hands on a tea-towel.

"You've done the swimming pool?"

"Yep, got that covered."

"There's a mother and baby group I usually go to with Amanda on Monday mornings. I'll drop the boys off at the Cricket Club where they're doing stuff for the kids this week - so I can leave some at the Club as well as the baby group. Will that help?"

"Wonderful! Thanks so much. Molly! Chas already emailed that you'd be coming. It's very pushchair-friendly."

"Yay!" chorussed the three boys, now joined by the bouncing giddy Alex.

"Did I hear my name?" Chas called through the open front door as he came round the front of the house from the side garden, Buster at his heels.

"Hi Chas! Thanks so much for volunteering to protect us all tomorrow! Or at least you were volunteered," smiled Tamsin.

"No trouble. We enjoyed the class a lot. You've certainly got a way with animals. When Charity recommended you I was on the fence. Not any more - it was great," he smiled.

"Thank you - that's music to my ears. And is Buster looking forward to the walk too?" asked Tamsin as the little dog sniffed her shoe.

"Ya-a-ay!" came the chorus again.

"I'll see you tomorrow so. We'll start on the next step towards Buster's first trick!"

"Yayayayay!" shouted the ever more excited children.

"Come on boys. Here Cameron, take these leaflets and put them by my car keys." Molly passed the wodge of flyers to him. "Then I won't forget them. Don't drop them all! Bye, Tamsin."

The boys scurried away and Tamsin said, "I didn't know you knew Shirley, Molly."

"Shirley who?"

"She was just leaving as I arrived. In a bit of a hurry."

"So that's what all the screeching tyre noise was. No? Don't know any Shirley. Was that the Shirley from the class?" she turned to Chas, who said, "That's the only Shirley I know of. I wonder what she was doing here."

Three more mysteries, thought Tamsin as she headed home again.

Susan didn't want to tell me something, Shirley doesn't want to speak to me at all, and Jean was behaving like a naughty schoolgirl. Whatever are they all hiding?

CHAPTER TWENTY

Tamsin still had a couple of hundred leaflets left, so she set off into town on Monday morning, Quiz with her. She didn't have favourites amongst her dogs, but ... she'd always found that the older a dog was the better they got. And when they started out with a sweet gentle nature, that only got sweeter and gentler as they aged. And easier to manage. So it always felt like a holiday when she took Quiz on a solo outing. So easy! Such a pleasure to have around. She was polite to strangers and happy to have them admire her. And she could always perform a trick if someone's heart needed melting, or a smile brought to their face.

And they both exchanged loving glances now as they walked the top road into town, Quiz's mouth opening slightly to accompany the smile her deep brown eyes were giving, and Tamsin's heart warming as it always did when she gazed at her dogs.

After doing two shoe shops, the bakery, the Library, the woo-woo and crystals emporium, the hiking store and the bicycle shop, she was down to fifty flyers, and found her feet taking her towards The Cake Stop. Of course! Why not?

As she looked for a table, having left almost all her stock of leaflets on the counter and one pinned on the noticeboard, a wagging tail caught her attention, and Muffin ran towards her, her lead trailing behind her.

"Muffy! Muffmuff!" called Charity urgently in a stage whisper, causing heads to turn.

Tamsin's hands were full with her tray of coffee, so Quiz picked up Muffin's lead and they went over to join her owner, who took Muffin on her lap between thanks and mock-scoldings.

"My dear, I was hoping to bump into you before tonight," Charity leant over confidentially, as Tamsin settled down with her coffee and Quiz lay down between them. "I've been doing some asking around, as I promised."

"Oh yes?" said Tamsin encouragingly, sighing with pleasure as she tasted her first mouthful of excellent coffee, trying to focus on that and not the absence of cake. She really had to cut down on cake. Cake two days running was probably a sin crying to heaven for vengeance. She couldn't risk that.

"There are very few people in the Trotley area who didn't employ Phil at some stage over the years. The only one who never has is Chas. Now," she said, even more confidentially, and leaning closer to Tamsin, "a little bird has told me that Phil had a run-in with Chas at the school."

"Oh?"

"I told you Phil was a bit of a busybody, always getting his nose into other folks' business? Well it seems that he made some suggestion that the baby didn't look like the boys, and that Chas should watch out for his wife."

"Oh wow. Bet that went down well," Tamsin took another swig of her coffee, noting that this was something Penelope had suggested too.

"Chas was livid! I don't know if he demanded Phil's dismissal - though who knows who else they'd get round here at the same rates - but he hasn't been up to the school again since." She leant back again, triumphant. "Hadn't been .." she corrected herself. "He can't go now."

"No indeed. Well, that would certainly cause Chas to resent Phil - hate him even. But he wouldn't need to kill him. If Chas has told everyone what Phil was suggesting, he couldn't even be blackmailed.

What a cauldron of seething emotions this beautiful countryside harbours!"

"Oh yes," said Charity with relish, breaking off two small pieces of her biscuit and passing one to Quiz and one to Muffin, who was now lying down beside her bigger friend.

"And there's more?" Tamsin raised an eyebrow as Charity was clearly not yet finished.

"There's more. It's something I learnt about Shirley."

"Where do you get all this stuff?"

"Oh, I couldn't possibly say," Charity looked coyly away, and smoothed her skirt over her knees. "But listen! *Apparently* Shirley had a cousin who went to Susan's mother for help with a - shall we say 'burgeoning' - problem, and when all was said and done, she ended up infertile. When she married and decided she did want a family, there was no family to be had."

"That's awful! I thought Susan said these things were safe?"

Charity leant back and folded her hands in her lap, in an 'I told you so' fashion.

"So Shirley would have had it in for Susan, I get that. But why might she murder Phil?"

"To point the finger, of course! To shift the blame onto Susan! Her chance to get even at last."

"Well that's a bit convoluted ... but I suppose it's possible. If your brain can conceive of murder, I suppose there's no limit to the mad things it may dream up." She reached down and stroked Quiz's ears for reassurance, like a child reaching for its special bear. Only this bear turned her head and gave Tamsin's hand a lick.

"But it doesn't get us much closer. Shirley said she left the car park first, you know. And Susan says *she* left first. Jean says Chas left first, and young Cameron says he heard another motor - that could have been a motorbike - leaving before them. All I know for a fact is that I left last. Well, almost last. Poor Phil was really the last to leave the car park that night." They both fell silent. "This was a person, Charity! This is where we live! It's all horrible. And I'm determined to see what I can find out."

As she left she handed Charity the last few flyers. "I'm sure you'll be able to find good homes for these, Charity. There's a lot riding on this walk on Wednesday!"

"Thanks - I've got a few places I can drop them in at. You've done a good job papering the town - I've seen them everywhere, counters, shop windows, noticeboards ... You have plenty of support and well-wishers, Tamsin."

Tamsin smiled broadly, "It'll be a fun event - see you tonight!"

As she arrived back home with Quiz she was given the long-lost treatment by her other two dogs, and Scruff who had been sleeping blamelessly in his crate. She kicked off her shoes, and played with them all for a couple of minutes while she fixed a sandwich for her lunch.

"I feel so virtuous not having cake," she told them as they listened with interest to her chatter, "and now I'm starving!"

They adjourned to the garden to enjoy her food, and to scatter some kibble on the grass for the dogs to snuffle out, doing their 'Sheep may safely graze' impression. And Tamsin's thoughts turned to Charity's revelations. There were nasty currents below the surface of this rural idyll, but she couldn't make any of them out. She decided to see what Feargal had discovered, so went inside again to ring him.

"I've heard something from Hawkins' department," he said with triumph. "They're closing in on Susan, according to my source." Tamsin could feel his nervous energy down the phone.

"That fits with what I've just learned," and Tamsin filled him in on the Shirley story, and threw in the info about Chas's grievance while she was at it.

"So you're thinking that Shirley did it in order to pass the blame onto Susan? Sounds a bit tenuous. I don't know what the police have got on our local witch, just that they're sniffing around there."

"What did they say about the break-in at Phil's cottage?"

"Treating it as vandals, apparently. Surprises me they don't see a connection with the murder. And all we found was that someone was ransacking that kitchen cupboard. Has Jean-Philippe any more intel on who those guys in the cafe were?"

"I don't think so. He said 'young men', and the only young men in all this are Gary, and Shirley's mystery man. I don't even know if they know each other. Oh, one of them had a motorbike, it seems."

"That motorbike again, eh?"

"There was a motorbike at Shirley's house when we visited," Tamsin said thoughtfully. "Ahh, it's all so confusing. I keep going round in circles and can't see anything clearly."

"It'll all become clear soon enough, it always does in the end. See you on your walk," and Feargal rang off, in a hurry as always.

And in complete contrast, that was when the languid Emerald wafted in, back from her individual class the other side of Malvern. "Glad to catch you in - I wanted to wish you well for this evening."

"Thanks - can I drop you somewhere when I go?"

"I'll be in the opposite direction! At The Cake Stop. I've got a private session too far away to walk to, so the client is coming there. Dead handy! My own private studio."

"Of course - sorry, my head's a bit scrambled at the moment ..."

"Not surprising. So tell me the latest!" and Tamsin filled her in with what she'd gleaned, to appropriate oohs and aahs from her rapt audience - of Emerald and on her lap the purring Opal, who managed to keep her large green eyes half-open .. for some of it, anyhow.

And it was not without trepidation that Tamsin got ready for her Trotley class, pocketing the keys that C.I. Hawkins had returned to her. She took Banjo with her - he was the most likely to react to anything untoward. And she took a little stool to teach Buster to hop up onto - the boys would love that, and it should entertain the others too. Once he can sit on it, I'll show them how to teach him a Sit Pretty, she thought - that'll be fun, and very cute!

She was pleasantly surprised when everyone turned up to class. She'd had visions of no-one coming, or just one or two, despite their assurances. But they all came. Could this mean anything? Would the murderer be sure to act natural and show up anyway? She needed to put this aside and focus on her job, thankful that she had the opportunity to do what she loved doing, however difficult the circumstances!

The students were mostly a bit uneasy. Except for Charity and Chas - Chas was busy minding his children, and Charity was happy as a sand-boy watching everyone else.

Jean looked prim and was careful to keep Mr.Twinkletoes well away from Shirley's Luke. And that, Tamsin felt sure, was not because she was afraid for her dog - Luke was a calm and gentle giant - rather that she wanted to keep her distance from his owner.

Shirley, for her part, looked very tense when she arrived, peering round the room anxiously. When she spotted Banjo on his bed near the table she seemed to relax. Had she been looking out for Scruff and expecting another barrage of barking?

Susan was more nervous and self-effacing than ever. She gripped Frankie's lead tight and kept darting looks at the others, though she was clearly avoiding looking at Charity.

Tamsin introduced Banjo, and explained that he would be doing some demos of the new games for them. Banjo was a sensitive soul, and Tamsin noticed that he would place himself on the other side of her whenever she was near Jean. Curiouser and curiouser. If only all these dogs could talk!

Chas's boys loved the trick of getting Buster to hop up onto his stool, and Cameron caught on quickly to how to get this to happen. "He's a natural," she said to Chas, "he'll be good at training."

"He's been drilling poor Buster all week since the last lesson. Joe tries his best, don't you Joey?" And Joe nodded seriously.

It wasn't until class was at an end and people were milling round the table eyeing the toys and pretty leads that Jean came out with her bombshell.

"Has anyone else had an anonymous phone call?" she asked, as she tried to choose between a blue and green tuggie and a yellow one.

"No!" gasped Susan, "that's awful! What did they say?"

"Just that they'd 'seen what I did'. Nonsense of course. Someone with a sick mind who enjoys scaring people. Gary showed me how to block the number - but there was no number. Somehow they did it without showing their number."

"Figures," said Shirley curtly. "It's not very anonymous if you expose your phone number."

"But who'd know how to hide their number? I certainly don't!" objected Jean, who had her dog in her free arm and was trying to keep him away from Shirley still.

"It's easy!" boasted Alex, "there's a code you put in and it hides your number!"

"And how do you know that?" asked Chas, a little perturbed at this revelation.

"I saw it on the telly."

"Yeah, on the telly," added Joe.

"How about you?" Jean persisted, "Have you had one, Chas?"

Chas looked at the expectant boys and quietly said no. Seems he did have a call, Tamsin thought, and didn't want to alarm the children.

"Have you had the police cross-questioning you?" asked Susan of everyone. They all nodded, and Alex and Joe started to bounce up and down in their excitement. "It's so awful," Susan went on, "to think that that could happen here, *in Nether Trotley!*" They glanced at each other, nodding again, the mood of enjoyment from the class dissipating into something more sombre.

It was dark by now, and as agreed, Chas shepherded everyone out to the car park, put on his headlights and kept his engine running while they all stowed their dogs and left, and then he left straight after them. Charity stayed to help sweep and pack up as before, happy to have the alert Banjo there to guard them.

Banjo knew Muffin well, and they had a friendly scamper around the sweeping before settling to some communal sniffing as Charity stacked the chairs.

And, of course, carried on with the latest gossip.

"I ran into Electra this afternoon," she began. "She told me the police were all over Phil's cottage. She had to go that way on her deliveries."

Tamsin blushed and turned away, saying, "Really?" and hoping her unsteady voice wasn't giving away her lie, she went on, "why was that?"

"Seems there's been a break-in there."

"Louts, I guess, taking advantage of the empty house?"

"Electra seemed to think there was more to it than that. The SOCOs were there, in their paper overalls. Must have been fingerprinting and all that kind of thing." She heaved a stack of chairs over to the wall. "And don't you think it's odd that Shirley seems to be the only person who hasn't had an anonymous call? I've had one, and it looks as though Chas has too. What about you?"

"Yep, I was honoured too. I did pass it on to Chief Inspector Hawkins. I assumed they'd do their magic with the phone company and find something out. Surely if Shirley was making the calls she'd claim that she'd had one too?"

"Mmm. But there's something odd about Shirley. You know she's got someone else living at her house at the moment?"

"Boyfriend? I saw him. He seems quite young. Has she a son?"

"If she has, she's kept him dark all these years …"

"Whoever he is, do you think he knows Jean's Gary?"

"Now that's a strange question. What are you thinking?"

Tamsin sighed. Should she keep this to herself? Why? The more people on the lookout the faster this was going to be solved. "Well … Jean-Philippe heard two young men talking about Phil in The Cake Stop. And they were saying that the secret lay in his cottage. So perhaps they were responsible for the break-in? And I wondered if it could have been Gary and Shirley's fella. Jean-Philippe said that one of them was wearing motorbike gear - and I saw a bike at Shirley's house."

"My! And I wonder what they can have been searching for?"

"You know what," said Tamsin as she cast an eye over the hall, got out the keys and hefted her box onto her hip, "it's time to put today to bed!"

And so they headed out to the car park, safely got into their cars, and left, with a cry of "See you on Wednesday!" ringing out from Charity's car window as they left.

CHAPTER TWENTY-ONE

"So, If you have a cast-iron recall and your dog is fine with other dogs, once we get away from the road we can gradually let them off lead." Tamsin was addressing the large group of walkers and dogs by the Common car park, projecting her voice so that they all had a chance of hearing her. "But if you're asked to catch your dog up, please do so, straight away! We want everyone to have a wonderful time. Perhaps you can space yourselves out a bit?" she said to two families whose terriers were eyeing each other with ill-concealed hostility. "Yes, I have plenty planned to make this a great day - recall games, races. And here's a special word for the children: Listen up, kids! Be sure to ask permission before you touch someone else's dog! Dogs have feelings too, just like you, and some of them are a little afraid of people they don't know. Oh, and don't forget to clean up carefully after your dogs - and join us for the refreshments at the end, when we get back here!"

Tamsin happily greeted many of her past students, complimenting them on how good their dogs were. They talked with enthusiasm about how much the classes had helped them - some were students who had been with her years ago. It gave her a very warm feeling, that she'd had such an effect on these people's lives.

She noticed Susan with Frankie standing a little apart - looking anxious as always - and she was fairly mobbed by Chas's boys who were wildly excited by the whole thing. Looking about she also saw Shirley, who appeared both frosty and worried at the same time, with Luke, and the young man she'd seen at her house. He was standing back a little as if wanting to dissociate himself from all this dog nonsense!

She got Scruff from the van and attached his lead to her walking belt so she could be hands-free, and so they set off, the crowd gradually spreading out and turning into a long column which reached halfway across the Common once they started moving. Tamsin stayed at the front - she had long since learned that if she stopped on a group walk, so did everybody else! She had Charity and Emerald spaced out along the crocodile of dogs and chattering families, and Feargal and his photographer Jeff were moving freely amongst the crowd. Feargal was chatting to people and admiring their dogs, and Jeff was snap-happy with his big camera. He was a jolly fellow and was clearly getting some excellent pictures of the children and their dogs, kneeling down to get good angles.

Close behind her were the two doctors from the Canal house near Bingham Parva with their old Labrador Jez, who Scruff was happily sniffing and wagging his tail at.

"I'm so glad you could come, Maggie," said Tamsin as she ruffled Jez's ear.

"Wouldn't have missed it for the world," laughed the lady doctor. "You've got quite a turnout!"

"Yeah, I'm delighted with the numbers. Will Jez be playing the games later on?"

"Definitely we'll have a go, won't we, Don?" she turned to her husband, who smiled widely.

They fell into step and admired the splendid mature parkland, Don pointing out the peep of a buzzard circling high above them. It was a glorious spring day, and everyone was in high spirits. Jeff appeared in front of Tamsin at one stage, just as she was helping a child with his small dog, showing him the safe way to hold the lead, and took several photos of her.

"These'll turn out well," he said - "good thing you got the weather for it!" and trotted off down the column to find more subjects for his pictures.

They'd been walking around for a good half hour when they reached a big open field. Tamsin had parked a load of plastic cones and other props there earlier on, and was relieved to see them all safe and that they hadn't been hi-jacked for some child's game. She chose a good spot and stopped there, and as she knew would happen, the column slowly changed shape and fanned out round her to listen. Funny how fluid crowds are! She divided them into rough groups, and spaced out the sets of markers well away from each other to avoid collisions.

That was when Scruff noticed Susan. He stiffened and stared. Tamsin was too preoccupied to take much notice and hurried him on so she could get the games going.

They started with some games to develop a fast recall which caused great amusement, as some dogs just raced about madly, while some others plodded to their owner's call. She thought the prize should go to the Basset Hound who simply lay down beside the first marker and refused to move another inch. Those who wanted to learn though were rewarded with some individual teaching, and there were some excellent and inspiring fast recalls from those who'd clearly put in the work.

She spotted little Jenny with her brother in his pushchair, both watching the dogs' antics keenly. "Lovely to see you here Jenny! Have you managed to say hello to some nice dogs?"

Jenny clasped her hands together and jumped about on the spot with delight.

"She's in heaven," smiled her mother. "She'd love a dog - but I couldn't manage a puppy as well as these two and holding down a job. Oh, I'm Val, by the way."

"Tamsin!" smiled Tamsin with a nod.

"You're welcome to join us on any of our walks Val, and maybe the time will be right one day for you to have a dog. It'll be worth waiting for, Jenny," Tamsin added.

Jenny reached over towards Scruff and said in a clear voice, "May I pet your dog?"

"Of course! Well remembered, Jenny."

"Isn't that the one ... it looks awfully like the one that nasty old man had," said Jenny's mother quietly as Scruff wagged his tail happily at the child, who was stroking his back very gently.

"Yes - he, er, wasn't able to look after him any more."

The woman's eyes widened. "He was the one who was killed!" she whispered.

"Yes, I'm minding his dog for now, till someone steps forward to claim him."

It was time to move on to the Egg and Spoon race. This was actually a Tennis Ball and Spoon race, and was even more entertaining than the recall games had been, as every time someone dropped the ball, one of the dogs would grab it and try to make away with it. Jeff had positioned himself at the far end of the course and was getting loads of action photos.

Buster had great fun with his tennis ball whenever one of the boys dropped it. At one stage he tripped Joe up, but Chas quickly lifted the child to his feet, dried his eyes, put the ball back in his spoon, and sent him scurrying ahead again.

The runners soon got canny though, and clamped the ball onto their spoon with a finger. It was the delight on the face of the children who tried so hard and raced so fast that everyone loved.

Jenny clapped her hands with glee as she watched the games with shining eyes. "She's got it bad," Tamsin said to Chas who was standing near her with his gang.

"I'm sure she'll wear her mother down one of these days, and get the dog she longs for," said Chas with a wry smile.

"Is that how it was for you?"

"Well, I've always liked dogs - but it was Cameron who forced us into getting Buster."

At that moment Cameron was introducing Buster to Scruff and - recognising a kindred spirit - Scruff instantly took to Buster, holding a long conversation with him, with much sniffing and tail-wagging, with softly open mouths. Tamsin noticed that he didn't seem worried about Chas or his family at all ...

She smiled and turned back to supervising the races. When all the children who wanted to play the game - and a few adults who were pushed into it by their families - had all had a go, the time was right to start heading back. The children were getting tired and starting to demand food. It had been a great day.

Charity started stacking the markers. "I'll deal with these, dear, you carry on." Scruff greeted his friends from class happily, as he and Muffin went nose to nose.

"Thanks, Charity - it seems to be going so well!"

At that moment there was a shout from the big copse at the side of the field. Tamsin startled and trotted up to find what the trouble was. The urgency in the shout had prompted Feargal to run towards the trees, with Jeff hot on his heels.

"There's this woman," a teenage boy said breathlessly, running towards them, "I think she's dead."

CHAPTER TWENTY-TWO

There was a woman alright, and it was Susan. But she wasn't dead. Yet.

"See that couple there with the black labrador?" Tamsin said to the lad, "Tall man in a blue jacket? They're doctors - run down and fetch them, would you?"

She exchanged glances with Feargal. "Susan," was all she said. "What's going on?!"

She spotted Frankie who was happily mooching about the woodland without appearing at all bothered, and she fetched him, picking up his trailing lead and attaching him to her belt along with Scruff.

"What happened?" demanded Tamsin of the doctors, hurrying back with the dogs, "This is ghastly!"

Susan stirred as Maggie examined her, asking questions to see how she responded. Don was on his phone calling an ambulance.

"Looks like she was banged on the side of the head," said Maggie, taking Susan's pulse.

"Could this be what did it?" asked Feargal, pointing to a short but stout branch lying across some nettles and comfrey.

"Don't touch it!" warned Don, making sure Jez didn't get any nearer to the prize stick which he already had his eyes on. "If it is, the police will want to have it."

"It could be, yes," said Maggie, looking from the stick to the bruise on Susan's head, and the shreds of bark caught in her hair.

Tamsin felt sick. "Look, can I go back to the walk? We need to get everyone moving on. Can you manage here till the ambulance comes?" she asked of the two doctors and Feargal. Jeff was busy taking photos of the scene.

"Maybe the police will want to talk to everyone," said Feargal. "Though most of them were completely focussed on the games."

"Well, whoever did it is hardly going to own up! And look - people are beginning to drift over. That lad has probably told everyone what he found. I need to move the children away ..."

"Sure, we'll stay here. Get them to the refreshments and let's hope the police get here fast."

Tamsin jogged back down the slope and headed the crowd off. "Food, everyone!" she said, to cheers from the children who instantly stopped nagging their parents and danced along behind Tamsin like the rats of Hamelin.

"They say someone's been killed!" a man pushed forward, squaring up to Tamsin. "This place isn't safe."

"It's fine, really! Someone tripped and fell in the woods there. She's ok, but the doctor called an ambulance just in case."

"I told you," said the man's wife, "It's just an accident."

"Come on! The grub's waiting!" Tamsin said to the impatient children following her, and the rest of the people gradually followed suit.

Back at the car park, everyone got stuck into the sandwiches and buns, with Emerald in charge of dishing them out and preventing too much thievery from small hands that tried to sneak extra.

Tamsin had to field a few questions about "the dead body", especially when they heard the wail of sirens and could see through the trees that an ambulance had driven right up the hill from the other end of the Common.

Jean was there as she had promised, many of the children fascinated with the tiny Mr.Twinkletoes. As Jean walked past the group, Tamsin had waved to her and did not fail to notice that Scruff smartly switched sides so that he was safe with her between him and Jean.

"Hi Electra!" Tamsin called out as she saw her deliver the last box of goodies to Emerald at the van. Electra looked past her to the mass of people near the van and shuddered, before giving a quick wave and jumping in her car to go.

"You wouldn't believe the number of sandwiches Jean helped herself to before I could stop her," said Emerald under her breath. "It's no wonder she can't walk well! What's the deal with the accident?"

"It's Susan," whispered Tamsin as she smilingly handed out some buns to the people just arriving at the van. "She's been hit on the head."

"That's her dog you've got there?"

"Yes, this is Frankie. Completely unbothered by the whole thing! Couldn't care less."

Right then, a police car arrived. The car park was so full that they had to stop on the road.

"Can you manage here? I'm going to try and head them off. Oh why does this keep happening to me?" she added as she turned from Emerald.

It was the same policemen that had attended the hall the previous week. "Can you drive round the other end?" asked Tamsin hopefully.

"It's you we want to talk to, Miss. What's happening here?"

"It's a dog walk I organised. The plan was to show that people who come to my classes don't get murdered. And now someone's been bashed on the head again. It's awful …"

"We'll need to get the details of all the people here, and any witnesses."

"I can give you a list of who's here, I think. And there weren't any witnesses. A young lad found her. But she's going to be ok, the doctors said. Fortunately they were here for the walk."

"The ambulance has just radio-ed in. They're taking her to Worcester General. She's just about conscious. We need to get over to the scene."

"You're best driving round the other side. It'll take you ages to walk and you can't drive that way - there are stiles."

"Don't mind saying, that's our chief suspect out of the frame. How long will you be here, Miss?"

"Oh, quite a while. I'll wait till everyone's gone and do any clearing up necessary. And you have my address. I'll expect your call." And she watched them get back into their car before turning back to the Common, switching her smile back on, and resuming chatting with her people.

Jeff had arrived with his camera and was amusing people while he took more photos.

"Where's Feargal?"

"Still up there," said Jeff. "Ambulance was leaving, so I came back down. Feargal wanted to guard the area till the police arrive. And of course he'll be on the spot if they find anything," he tapped his nose and smiled. "The doctor's just coming over," he added, snapping a photo of the approaching Maggie and Don with Jez trotting along between them.

"Thank you so much for your help," Tamsin said to Maggie as she strode towards them. "What's the story?"

"She'll live, but she'll have quite a headache."

"Is it possible it was an accident? I've no idea why she'd be up there in the copse anyway - I didn't think Susan was the adventurous sort."

"It is just conceivable that she could have tripped and hit her head. The SOCOs will have to find out where the bark in her hair came from. I kept some of it and gave it to that journalist chappie. He's waiting there for the police, so he said he'd give it to them."

"There are plenty of trees she could have hit her head on up there. She couldn't have faked it, could she? Done it herself?"

"That would be hard, but I wouldn't say impossible," said Don, stroking his chin thoughtfully. "There have been cases where people have deliberately hurled themselves against a wall to make it look like an attack. Is she mentally disturbed?"

"I'm beginning to think everyone connected with this case is! And I'm wondering why anyone would want to attack her. Of course, if she did it herself it may be a way to deflect suspicion from her. Apparently she's the no.1 suspect for the murder."

"Perhaps she knows something?" interjected Maggie, "Isn't that the usual reason there's a second attack?"

Tamsin felt her stomach lurch. "If that's the case, we've got this mad murderer still on the loose. I wish the police would stop him before .." she bit her lip, unwilling to follow that thought.

"I'm sure they're working hard behind the scenes. They do it all methodically their own way. They have to collect evidence - it takes time."

"Well, I guess you know a lot about it all, given what your day-job is," Tamsin smiled at Maggie, only now remembering that she was a pathologist.

"Don't worry, they get there in the end. Now we must be off, come on Jez - and thanks for a lovely walk. We really enjoyed it - count us in for the next one."

"Next time I sincerely hope you won't be called upon to do anything but juggle tennis balls on spoons!"

Tamsin felt calmed by the doctors' professional attitude, and went back to find Charity loading the plastic markers into the van - now almost empty of food - and people organising their tired dogs and children back into their cars, with lots of cheery waves.

"Seems people have made new friends," Emerald walked up beside her. "Your walk was a great success! Apart from one thing, that is ..."

"'Other than that, how was the play, Mrs. Lincoln?'" Tamsin grimaced.

"Now dear, don't you worry. No-one died - maybe it was an accident anyway?" Charity said cheerily.

"I'd like to think it was. But I fear it wasn't ... Thanks for all your help, Charity - you're a brick."

"Let's go home," said Emerald, "We can clean up the van tomorrow. We need coffee!"

"Or something stronger. And we have yet another mouth to feed here."

"You'll have to stop murdering people and stealing their dogs," laughed Emerald as they clambered into the van.

"Not funny!" said Tamsin, as she checked her phone for messages. "Feargal's coming round too when he's finished up there. Let's go."

CHAPTER TWENTY-THREE

Feargal arrived at Tamsin's house half an hour or so later. He was full of his news, and as ever was glad to accept the offer of coffee.

Tamsin was happy to let him lead the discussion - she was exhausted! Tired physically after all the effort of the walk, and wrung out emotionally.

"So Susan, Shirley, Chas, Jean and Charity were all there," he said.

"Not Charity!" said Tamsin, "Surely we can count Charity out?"

"Let's leave her right in there for the moment. And think of Susan's accident. It seems to me there are three possible explanations:

One, that it was an accident. But why was she up in the woods in the first place? Two, that it was self-inflicted, in order to place the blame for Phil's murder elsewhere. Or three, that it was attempted murder to silence Susan. And, of course, was it the same perp for both attacks?"

"None of those are good from my point of view. Even if it had been an accident, what was she doing in the woods?"

"Needed a wee?" said Emerald hopefully.

"Highly probable. And self-inflicted," Tamsin went on, "Don suggested it was possible, but not awfully likely. She could just have thrown herself at a tree trunk ... But I suppose if that stick you saw matches her head-wound then that would count that out."

"The police bagged it and took it," said Feargal. "SOCO had just arrived like an army of paper-clad ants as I was leaving."

"It does look deliberate, and I guess the police think that too. But who would do that? And why?"

"And why didn't they finish her off?" chipped in Emerald.

"Let's take them one by one," Feargal leant back in his chair. "Jean. She didn't go on the walk, did she?"

"No, she says she can't walk far - and that tiny dog of hers probably can't either," said Emerald.

"You'd be surprised!" said Tamsin, "Chihuahuas are pretty active when they're allowed to be."

"Anyway, I saw her arrive when the main walk was just coming back from the games."

"Did she have that son of hers with her?" Feargal put in quickly.

"Nope. It was just her. She could have dropped him off the other end of the Common?"

"She certainly could. And gone to collect him again when she left," mused Tamsin.

"We know Susan was on the walk. But she didn't take part in any of the games?" Feargal got them back on track.

"She didn't. But I wouldn't have expected her to, really. She was on her own a lot of the time, not chatting with the others, you know?"

"And Shirley? Where was she?"

"Well, that was a bit odd. I didn't expect her mystery man to come with her. She does get pulled around by Luke, but he likes other dogs and he's no trouble. She didn't need help."

"I saw him standing about at the back looking bored while the games were on. I wonder ... and Chas?"

"He was much involved in the games. All three children wanted to have a go at something. Fortunately Buster is full of energy and enjoyed flying about snatching tennis balls, so one of his kids was involved in each run."

"He wouldn't have abandoned the children anyway, would he?" asked Emerald.

"No, I'm sure he wasn't involved."

"And lastly, there's Charity."

"I really find it hard to believe Charity could have done any of this. She was certainly around during the games. I saw her helping a couple of the younger children and explaining to them not to put the lead in the hand holding the spoon. And she was last to leave the hall that night, just before me. And you know what? Whatever she may be capable of doing to a person, I can't imagine her leaving Scruff like that. She'd have put him in the car or something."

"Same goes for leaving Frankie loose, I suppose?" asked Emerald.

"Mm-hm," nodded Tamsin.

Feargal craned his neck to see out of the front window as a car pulled up. "Ah, it's Jeff. I asked him to drop over - you're going to love what he's got!"

Jeff arrived, still carrying his camera. "Thanks, yes - I could murder a cup of coffee!" he said, before adding, "Hmm, perhaps not the most tactful remark ..."

Feargal laughed and said, "Just look at this!" with glee, beckoning Jeff forward with his camera. They all gathered round as Jeff scrolled through the thumbnails on the back of his camera.

"It's these ones here," he said, as the pictures showed the games taking place. "I got round the far end so I could get all the people in shot as well as the runners, and that meant I had a view of the copse - or rather, my camera did! I wasn't looking up there at all."

He flipped through a few of the photos till he got to one, and he paused. "There's Susan going into the wood with her big lummox of a dog, this one you've got here." He nodded to Frankie who wagged his tail appreciatively. They could see Susan glancing round nervously as she entered the copse.

"Know who this is?" asked Jeff as he flipped a few pictures on and showed a man in a hoodie sidling out of the copse.

"A Hoodie again," murmured Feargal.

Jeff flicked to the next image, which showed the hooded man with his hands in his pockets, sauntering away from the copse and the crowd, towards the other exit. Then the pictures focussed on the games again.

"Show me the hood guy again," said Tamsin, peering at the little image as Jeff magnified it as far as he could in the viewing pane. "Quite thickset. No idea. He's turned away in that image," she said, "and in the other one his head is bent under his hood."

Jeff scrolled on through several more images and showed the frightened boy come bursting out of the copse, then another picture as he ran towards the people, shouting and waving his arms.

"What's the time frame?" asked Feargal.

"From Susan going in till Mr.Hoodie left is just over three minutes. It was another eleven minutes before the boy appeared."

"Did you show these to the police?" Emerald asked, hoisting Opal onto her lap.

"Yes. And I've been up at the station transferring them to their computer. I didn't want them confiscating my camera or the card, so I offered to go up there. That's why I'm only arriving with you now. Feargal told me to get here as soon as I could. Thanks, two please!" he added, as Emerald held up the sugar bowl questioningly and handed him his coffee.

"So this man - looks youngish - seems to have attacked Susan," said Tamsin. "There are only two young men associated with this case -"

"Jean's Gary and Shirley's mystery man!" interrupted Feargal.

"Why would either of them want to hurt Susan?"

"And why didn't they finish her off?" Emerald said again.

"Assuming they only meant to knock her out and not kill her, perhaps it was a warning. Perhaps she's poking her nose in?" Feargal offered.

"'Poking her nose in.' That's what they all said about Phil," said Emerald.

"Yeah," said Tamsin, "Susan said it. And who else …? Ah yes, the Furies said it too. That's Dodds & Co to you," she said to the puzzled-looking Jeff. "Perhaps it's an occupational hazard in a small hamlet, minding other people's business?"

"Perhaps ..." said Emerald thoughtfully, stroking Opal's purring head, "They were both poking in the same business? Phil was stopped, and Susan warned off."

"And maybe Phil should have been warned off, but hitting the old injury on his head caused his death, and that wasn't intended?"

"They say it wasn't a very hard blow to his head - just unfortunate." Feargal said reflectively. "I wonder ... perhaps the first strike was one of your students, Tamsin, and the second was one of those men."

"Or maybe .. just maybe," said Emerald, "*someone else* attacked Susan. And Mr.Hoodie just came across her, or saw what happened, and had nothing to do with it? A Red Hoodie Herring!"

"Oh Emerald, you're removing our suspects as fast as we find them!" complained Tamsin. Her phone started ringing, and as she reached to turn it off, something prompted her to answer it. She walked out to the kitchen to talk, and came back a few moments later.

"That was Sally. She's Susan's niece. Apparently she's visiting and has been at Susan's the last few days. The police rang her."

"And?" prompted Jeff.

"She's just at the hospital, and she wanted to know what happened to the dog. Says her life wouldn't be worth living if she couldn't reassure Susan that he's safe."

"She sounds thoughtful," said Emerald.

"I was able to tell her she could put Susan's mind at rest on that. Anyhoo, she plans to be back in Nether Trotley within the hour, so I said I'd drop Frankie over then. Anybody up for a ride?"

"Wild horses and all that!" said Feargal keenly. "Another person to grill!"

"I have a class to get to," said Emerald sadly, "but I'll look forward to hearing all about Sally and what she thinks. I wonder if she's a witch too ..."

"I gotta get away," said Jeff, gathering his kit together and getting up. "Thanks for the coffee - and I got lots of good photos. Tell you what, after they've taken what they want for the paper, I can give you the card and you can help yourself, for your website. Least I can do to help out. A credit would be nice, though ..."

"Jeff, that's amazing! Thank you."

Moonbeam detected the imminent departure of her people and watched attentively in case it meant it was dinnertime. "Later Poppet," said Tamsin as she fetched her keys.

And after chatting a bit longer, then settling the dogs, Feargal and Tamsin set off for Susan's house to see what they may discover. Things were beginning to move very fast.

CHAPTER TWENTY-FOUR

It had been a long day, but Tamsin and Feargal were re-invigorated as they arrived at Susan's house. Frankie knew where he was immediately and was keen to get out of the van and go in. He greeted Sally enthusiastically at the door, and she looked as though she was going to send them on their way with brief thanks, when Tamsin said, "Hey, may we come in? I really want to hear how Susan is doing, and you just might have something you can tell us that can help nail her attacker."

"I'm sure you're keen to get whoever it is behind bars?" added Feargal.

"Yes, of course, I'm sorry ... I'm a bit distracted by all this. Come in!" Sally led them to the living room and said, "Hospital tea is awful - I'm dying for a decent cuppa. How about you?"

Tamsin knew well that refusing hospitality sent the wrong message, so despite being full to the gunwales with coffee, she enthusiastically agreed.

Feargal took the opportunity to look around the room while Sally was in the kitchen. It all looked much the same to Tamsin as it had when she'd last visited. Even down to a stretched-out Frankie on the hearth rug. He was clearly very happy to be home after his unexpected adventure.

Feargal peered closely at the photos, just as Tamsin had done, then fingered some of the books on the bookshelf. They were mostly very old, apart from a few battered paperbacks of bodice-rippers, and had words like "Apothecary" and "Physick" on their dark red spines.

"Are these where the recipes come from?" he asked Sally as she returned to the room with a tea tray.

"There, and from Susan's head. I guess she has them written down somewhere, but a lot of them she knows off by heart. There's a lot of skill involved - it depends what time of year you harvest the plant, how strong it'll be. Even how old the plant is, in years."

"Goodness, I never thought of that!" said Tamsin, accepting the mug of tea.

"So different combinations of herbs will work differently too, depending on the season, the weather, and even the place they're grown in."

"It's more complicated than I thought ... Susan'll be longing to get her own potions rather than whatever the Health Service is giving her, I'll bet!" Feargal said. "How long is she staying in?"

"They reckon I can probably collect her tomorrow. They want to keep her under observation overnight, do those concussion tests again in the morning."

"'Who's the prime minister' sort of questions?"

"Yes, and what year it is and that kind of thing. Fortunately she was all clear when I visited her. Quite lucid."

"And what does she say happened? Was it an accident? Did she trip over a root?"

"That she can't remember clearly. She's pretty surefooted when it comes to walking through undergrowth - she spends half her life in the garden here. She just remembers walking into the wood, then - nothing else till she woke properly in the hospital."

"Why did she go there?" Tamsin leant forward in her chair.

"She didn't say. My guess is a call of nature," Sally said, a little primly, as she glanced at Feargal. "She's not that young any more, you know."

"And does she have any idea who would have attacked her - if it *was* an attack?"

"Not a clue. She said some dark things about Phil's murder, and wondered if she's next on the list. But she has no idea why she should be," Sally added defiantly.

"I heard a whisper ..." said Tamsin, "about someone suffering bad side-effects from one of Susan's mother's remedies - that'd be your grandmother, right?"

"There have always been whispers. Like now, they'll blame the doctor if someone dies. But her remedies have been tried and tested down the centuries - they're fine. I use them myself!"

"So you don't think someone may have it in for Susan's family, and finally saw their opportunity to have a go?" asked Feargal.

"Not awfully likely is it, after all these years? Gran has been dead for a good while now. If it was something she administered .. Susan only does simple remedies you see, so they couldn't blame her." Tamsin guessed this was Sally's way of saying she didn't dish out abortifacients any more.

"Maybe someone thought they'd take their opportunity and it would be blamed on whoever did for Phil," mused Tamsin, hoping that floating an idea might draw out some more information.

"I really don't know. I've never lived in Nether Trotley myself, though I've visited here frequently, of course, down the years. So I don't know the factions who may be involved."

"You're a sharp person," prompted Feargal in his most flattering voice, "what do *you* think?"

"Well ..." Sally thought hard then decided to carry on. "I've never had much time for those boys who used to run amok in Baynton .. rough lot they've always been. My mother forbade me to talk to them."

"You think one of them killed Phil, then banged Susan on the head - either to kill her too or warn her off? They must think she saw something."

"Maybe she did, and didn't realise it ..." said Feargal thoughtfully. "And by the Baynton boys I take it you're including Jean's son, Gary?"

"Always a troublemaker, Gary." Sally folded her arms. Then into the silence she added, "It's just as well I'd planned this visit - Susan will need looking after for a while," and she stood to indicate the end of the interview.

"You'd just arrived had you? What a thing to greet you!"

"Oh no, I've been here for a couple of weeks."

"Really? How did I miss you when I visited Susan before?"

"I was out," said Sally, rather too quickly. "At the supermarket down at the Retail Park. Yes," she nodded, to drive the point home.

"You didn't fancy coming to the class with her the night before?"

"Actually, I was meeting up with some old friends at the pub." She smiled sweetly as she held the door open for them.

They thanked Sally for the tea and her time, and asked her to let them know if there was any change in Susan's recovery, as Tamsin bade a cheery farewell to Frankie. "He hasn't been fed this evening, by the way."

"Well, that didn't tell us too much," said Tamsin as they drove her van back to her house and Feargal's car. "Except .. I wonder if someone else had reason to hate Susan's family. I don't see how the two attacks can be connected ... I mean, if Susan had wanted to get rid of Phil she could have easily done it with one of her back-pain remedies."

"It's got to be connected. I don't see how they *can't* be connected." Feargal paused to let a noisy tractor go by. "There are no coincidences. Didn't Hercule Poirot say that?"

"Miss Marple, I think? We have a hard act to follow!" laughed Tamsin. "Ok. So supposing Gary wanted to bump Phil off for some reason we don't yet know about. And he thinks Susan saw him do it. Or she's said something that points to him. From all accounts he'd be well able to dispatch her. So why didn't he?"

"Must have been a warning," as you suggested.

"Why might Gary have had it in for Phil? He's just back on leave, so maybe it's something that happened some time ago?" She looked at the sign on the noticeboard they were passing as they went through another small village. It announced the summer fete and flower show. "Here!" she said quickly, "I wonder if Jean had to stop running all the Women's Institute lectures and the Gardening Society flower things - not because of her bad leg, but because Phil had seen something!"

"That she was fixing the prizes or something?"

"Maybe poisoning other gardeners' exhibits ... maybe using an untraceable poison of Susan's ... hey, maybe we're on to something here!"

"From what you told me before, Jean is a doting mother. Perhaps her son is a doting son in return."

"And wants to wreak justice with a bit of violence while he's away from the military hot spots he's been in. War must play havoc with your moral code if you're a bit bent to start with?"

"Let's think on this. I'll do a bit of ferreting around in the Mercury files, on upsets in flower competitions. Right now I have to get your story written or we'll miss the deadline.

"Oh Lord, my triumphant Publicity Walk has so backfired."

"Don't worry, I'll keep the attack out of the story. But I can't guarantee it won't appear elsewhere in the online edition."

"I did have a few cancellations straight after the first disaster, and I'm getting fewer enquiries than I'd expect at this time of year. But that was a great expression of loyalty from all those people on the walk - let's hope your nice positive piece will attract some more. It *was* a fun walk!"

"Jeff's photos will do a lot - he's very good."

As they arrived back at Feargal's car, Tamsin said, "Do you suppose Sally could have had anything to do with this. I'd no idea she was staying with Susan at the time."

"And it's very odd how quickly she jumped in with an answer for you. Though why she'd need to lie about the day *after* the murder, I can't imagine. Maybe she was looking for evidence at the car park?"

"It was all still taped off with police tape on the Tuesday. She wouldn't have been able to get close - although, come to think of it, it's so remote no-one would have seen her. Maybe there was something she wanted to retrieve ...?"

"Emerald was trying to diminish our number of suspects - looks like we've got ourselves another one!"

"I'm going to sit down and write everything out this evening. I've got to prep for a couple of home visits tomorrow, but I'll fit it in somehow. Any news from your police mole?"

"Nothing new. They seem to be dragging their feet a bit. Hawkins is not really that bothered. He's hoping to get his retirement without a blot on his copy-book. As this case seems to be quite convoluted, maybe he'd like to let his successor deal with it."

"We'll have to bat on then. I can't have this hanging around over me for months. I'll go bust ..."

CHAPTER TWENTY-FIVE

"Ahhh," sighed Tamsin as she sank into the comfy armchair in the front window of The Cake Stop, her home visits done for the day. Banjo sat on the mat she'd put down for him beside her chair, safely out of the way of any other customers, and rested his chin on her knee, gazing up at her.

"I've got something for you, don't worry," she smiled, as she pulled a food-toy filled with kibble and some peanut butter out of her bag for him. Banjo took it very gently from her hand and turned round and lay down on his mat to get started on it.

"Tired?" asked Kylie, as she brought a tray over to the table, bearing a large Cappuccino and a huge slice of carrot cake - today's special from the Furies.

Tamsin sighed as she looked at it - her resolve not to have cake hadn't lasted beyond catching sight of it at the counter.

"Yeah, big day yesterday."

"How did it go? Nobody could move in Malvern without seeing one of your posters! Did you have a good turnout?"

"Massive! That was really good. But there was an incident … I'm surprised you haven't heard, being as this is the hub of all news in the area."

"I'm only just in, and we've been busy. Oh, Jean-Philippe needs me - tell me more in a minute …" and she flipped her tea-towel over her shoulder, flicked her pink hair out of her eyes, and sped back to the serving area.

Tamsin dangled a hand down to touch Banjo's thick white mane, leant back in the chair and closed her eyes. Her home visits had gone really well. One had been to Jez's owners, the doctors.

"I had another look at my notes on your murder victim," Maggie had said. "Just wanted to compare with what I'd seen of Susan's head."

"And?" Tamsin was wide-eyed, astonished that she was privy to this information, and hesitant to say anything that may stop the flow.

"Not the same attacker, in my opinion."

"Really? That is very interesting …"

"No more details for you, but just thought you may have a use for that information. Not that I'm suggesting you interfere with the police investigation, of course …"

"Of course," said Don, tossing Jez a piece of sausage as he lay perfectly on his mat as requested, without budging - despite his thumping tail.

"Of course," echoed Tamsin, mouth still slightly open.

She opened her eyes now and saw the inviting cake, and could resist it no longer. The sugar rush of the icing did wonders to relax her, and she was feeling quite energised by the time her friend Jean-Philippe came over and joined her. As was proper he greeted Banjo cordially but without bending over him, and the greeting was briefly returned with a gentle blink before Banjo carried on mining his food-toy.

"Those guys were in again - thought you'd like to know."

"I seem to be Central Clearing for information pertaining to local violent crime today," smiled Tamsin. "Tell me more .."

Jean-Philippe leant forward in his seat. "They were arguing quite urgently with each other. Perhaps thieves are falling out?"

"Any idea who they are yet?"

"Yes."

"Yes?!" squawked Tamsin, "Spill the beans!"

"While they were here, that woman Shirley - the one your new dog barked at .."

"Scruff."

"Scruff?"

"Scruff. The old man's dog."

"*Ah oui* - well, she came in again. She just stood in the doorway and stared at them. The smarter-looking of the two looked over to her, rather guiltily I thought ... or maybe imagined ... and gave a slight wave. Then she left again."

"So maybe he's that young man from her house. The plot thickens," she smiled. "And I wonder if the other one is Gary?"

"Gary?"

"The son of one of the other students."

"Short square chap, very muscly and tough-looking. Rather belligerent expression."

"The mother is short and broad too. Sounds a typical Squaddie - that would fit alright. We're thinking," she leant forward and spoke quietly, "that maybe Phil had something to do with unseating her from her special position in the Women's Institute. That maybe she'd been up to no good with the flower competitions. She used to win them all, apparently. And that maybe Phil knew and was blackmailing her. It seems the sort of thing he did."

"Now that sounds entirely possible. If it happened. Though how someone could get murdered over a flower competition beggars belief."

"You aren't reckoning with the fervour of the amateur enthusiast! Feargal is checking all that in the Mercury records. He's bound to turn up something." She sat back again in her armchair, running her finger through the last squashy morsel of icing on her plate, then sucking it thoughtfully. "I wonder what the connection with Shirley's man is, though."

"And who *is* Shirley's man? Boyfriend?"

"Bit young. My guess is son. Maybe he used to kick around with "the Baynton gang" as a schoolboy. They were local riff-raff, it seems. But no-o," added Tamsin slowly, "Charity said Shirley only moved here a few years ago. And she does have a bit of a Brummy accent. How about the guy you saw?"

"Couldn't hear. But then," he winked, "you English all sound the same to me."

Tamsin grinned back at her friend.

"Are your classes always so incestuous?" Jean-Philippe smiled his crooked smile, reminding Tamsin of how very attractive he was in all his Frenchness.

"The ones in town aren't. This is obviously the hazard in moving into deep countryside!"

"You know someone, or someones, who may know more?"

"Charity? She seems to know everything."

"Yes - her and the Furies. Indomitable, the lot of them. Why don't you go fishing there again?"

"I will." Tamsin said slowly. "Has Charity been in today?"

"Talk of the *diable!*" Jean-Philippe smiled broadly as he rose to his feet, the door opened and Charity made an entrance, laden with shopping bags, led by Muffin who was excited to see so many friends, potential friends, and victims of her affection, all in one place.

He called Charity over and offered her the seat he had vacated.

"Oh thank you, Jean-Philippe," she flustered, "*Merci!* Oh, Muffy-muff, behave nicely now," she chattered as Muffin strained to see what Banjo had. The food-toy was now empty and Tamsin scooped it up before there could be any argument over it.

"Will I hold Muffin while you order, Charity?"

"Oh thank you, my dear, thank you. *Merci encore!*" Charity laughed as she handed the lead over and went to the counter, nodding to people and mouthing hellos as she went.

"She's in fine fettle today," mused Jean-Philippe as he departed. "Have fun!"

Tamsin watched Charity's bird-like form as she worked the room. She really does seem to know everyone, she thought. And by the time she arrived back with her coffee, she found her little dog firmly ensconced on Tamsin's lap.

"I brought this over for you to see," she said as she sat down, holding out the latest edition of the Malvern Mercury for her. "The second edition just arrived."

"Ooh thanks! I must buy a copy. Let's see now ..." and she flipped through the pages till she found a double-page spread of sunny images of happy children, smiling parents, and even happier dogs. "These are really good! That Jeff knows how to wield a camera alright. And Feargal's written a lovely report ..." She scanned the piece quickly. "This should go some way to restoring my reputation!" She flipped back to the front page of the paper, and spotted a small paragraph warning of the dangers of going off the footpaths after a woman was found unconscious in woods after a fall. 'Foul play is not suspected'. The police obviously want to keep a lid on that." She turned back to the centre spread, "Oh here you are, Charity!" she pointed at the large picture.

Charity adjusted her glasses and peered at the page. "And look who's behind me," she said, pointing.

"Me! And Scruff. Actually he has a strange expression on his face - oh! He's looking past you .. At that group to the left - Chas and his wife are at the front of it, with the baby's pushchair. Well, well. I was watching out for his reactions on the walk. He wasn't mad about Shirley, but we know that already. Susan never got near enough for me to see what Scruff really thought of her. Maybe the rest of the photos caught something?"

"Were you hoping for an identification parade with your chief witness?" smiled Charity. "I don't know why he wouldn't like Chas, who seems to play with Buster and his boys a lot ... Do you think it was Molly he had actually spotted? Now why would she upset the little dog ..." she mused. "I did notice that Scruff seemed quite happy with Frankie, once you had him in tow."

"True, but I remember now, he did react to catching sight of Susan. It was just as we were beginning the games. He went quite rigid and stood stock still. But I just don't think he's a reliable witness," sighed Tamsin. "Too much to hope for, to expect him to point the paw for us. But it was worth a try. My bet is that the whole evening was so traumatic for him that he's triggered by the sight of all the people he met there. Except for you. He seems to have taken a shine to you."

Charity beamed. "Dogs always seem to like me," she said with pride.

"Tell me, Charity, have you seen the Furies since? They did a grand job with the refreshments. I'll be dropping round there tomorrow to settle up."

"I have," Charity beamed even more. "And, they told me something interesting about Shirley."

"Yes?"

"It seems that she has a bit of a secret history. The young man who was with her on the walk - well, it seems he's her son."

"Got it in one!" said Tamsin.

Charity seemed a little crestfallen that her news was not entirely news, but went on, "and he's just back after having been away for quite a long time ... Electra wondered if it was 'at Her Majesty's Pleasure'."

"A long-stay hotel with bars on?"

"That's what Electra seemed to think. Seems she overheard them talking in the supermarket. He was being difficult about the shopping and said something like, 'anything's better than the food I've had to put up with for the last seven years'."

"Maybe he wasn't in prison, but in the army? Maybe that's why he and Gary are thick as thieves?" And she passed on what Jean-Philippe had told her.

"Two disenchanted tough guys with mothers to protect. Could be a potent combination."

"And yet, if they're trained killers, why did they make a hash of Susan?"

"How is Susan? Any news?"

"Seems she'll be home tomorrow."

"I must drop round and see if she needs anything," said Charity, living up to her name.

"No, she's ok. She has her niece Sally there. That's who I left Frankie with. She's been staying with her for a while."

"Really? I had no idea. She's been keeping low. She used to visit frequently as a girl."

"I don't know why she's there now. Just a family visit, I suppose. But I wonder why you didn't know. You know everything!"

"My radar scanners must need oiling," smiled Charity. "Now, I wonder …"

Tamsin's ears pricked up.

"She's about the same sort of age as these other two we've been talking about. They probably knew each other from way back. She and Gary, that is."

"She made a point of saying that her mother forbade her to mix with Gary …"

"And how many girls listen to what their mother says where boys are concerned, hmm?"

"Very true - perhaps she was 'protesting too much'. Perhaps there's history."

"And we never knew anything about Shirley's son. She arrived in Malvern alone."

"Was he never there? No leave from the services?"

"That's true. Seems to point to the prison hypothesis after all."

"That's another thing for Feargal to unearth. So I wonder how he knows Gary?" Tamsin stretched again and reached for Banjo's lead. "My head's spinning with all this. The solution is going to be so obvious when we finally find it."

"We're going to find the solution then?"

"Oh yes, we most certainly are!" said Tamsin as she stood up, tipping Muffin back onto the floor. "Let's-go, Ban-jo!" she chanted, like a sports fan, as she gathered her things and set off, head held high.

CHAPTER TWENTY-SIX

"So let me get this straight," said Emerald, her legs crossed under her, a pencil poised over the back of the large envelope she'd fished out of the waste paper basket. "Shirley could have been blackmailing Susan over what happened to her cousin after taking Susan's mother's magic potion. And Phil could have been blackmailing Chas about his baby."

"Bit thin, aren't they," said Tamsin dejectedly.

"Yeah, 'fraid so. Chas told everyone what Phil had said, and laughed it off. So no danger of blackmail there."

"And why would Shirley suddenly seek revenge, for someone else, years too late?"

Emerald tapped her teeth with the pencil. "What about Sally and Gary? Perhaps they had a hatred of Phil from way back when they were kids playing pranks, and Phil was nasty to them. I can imagine that festering for years - especially when they're both away from the area."

"Oh! And we forgot about Jean! Maybe Phil was blackmailing her because he knew something about her flower show wins? I've yet to hear back from Feargal about that."

"In that case, Gary may have been happy to ride in like a white knight to defend his mother as it gave him the chance for payback for the slights and bullying suffered from Phil years ago."

"That's certainly a possibility. And the most likely scenario we've managed to come up with. Remember Cameron thought he heard an engine leaving before them - could have been a bike."

"Hmm," Emerald started to doodle flowing shapes round what she'd written down. "Where does that leave us with Susan's attack?"

"How about ….." began Tamsin slowly, "How about Sally? Maybe she wanted to deflect any possible suspicion from Gary - her old heart-throb - and whacked her aunt round the head herself?'

"What for?" demanded Emerald.

"Just to spread suspicion around. Gary wasn't at the walk - as far as we know. Maybe he has an alibi for that afternoon, which the police will uncover as soon as they go to clap him in irons."

"So you think it was Gary and Sally?"

"Oh, I dunno," sighed Tamsin. "I do think the Susan attack is a bit of a side-issue. Hey! How about this: Chas whacked Phil over the head in a tantrum, following a quick argument with him in the car park. Had no idea it would kill him. Then, Gary boasts about Phil getting his come-uppance at last, and Sally thinks he did it. So she manufactures another attack when she knows Gary will have an alibi. Whaddya think?"

"It's about as far-fetched as all the other ideas we've come up with."

Tamsin sighed gloomily. "Fancy a walk up on the Hills? Blow the cobwebs out of our brains?"

"Sure! I don't have a class this evening, so I'm a bit under-exercised. I'll go and put on some shoes."

"There's still a couple of hours of light - we can catch that lovely part of the day."

"The gloaming?"

"We'll be roamin' in the gloamin'!"

The dogs, having heard the magic word 'walk', despite it being buried in a sentence, started to spin and scurry about the place. Scruff joined in, not slow to pick up on the excitement.

Quiz rummaged in the toybox, grabbed a frisbee and nudged Tamsin's leg with it.

"Ok, Quiz," she laughed, "I'll bring our new frisbug with us." And she folded the soft fabric disc and slid it into her back pocket.

The beauty of the Malvern Hills soon put both of them back into good humour. Emerald danced ahead up the hill toward the Worcestershire Beacon, while Tamsin puffed behind more slowly, cursing the Furies for their irresistible cakes. It was a beautiful evening and they could see for miles on this visit; see across the patchwork of fields and woodland, dotted with farmhouses and villages, a thin plume of smoke rising from a chimney here and there; see the ranges of hills spreading out before them.

When they reached the top of the Beacon, they leaned over the toposcope - that metal map on top of the pillar marking the triangulation point - which had pointers to everything they could see. The furthest was the Black Mountains in Wales, a delicate misty blue today.

"I think that's Bromyard Downs over there," Emerald pointed excitedly, as she consulted the arrows on the toposcope.

"Another place with lovely walks."

"Do you see the whole country in terms of dog walks?" laughed Emerald.

"Of course! All the bits in between are just how to get from one to another," and she swept her windblown hair out of her eyes.

"You get plenty of fresh air up here," said Emerald, doing the same thing, and tucking her hair behind her ears.

"It's a wonderful place to refresh your mind," added Tamsin. "Clears your head. Gets things back in proportion."

"And even on a lovely evening like this there aren't many walkers about. We only passed a few people on our way up - plenty of space for everyone."

Once the dogs had snuffled all the rocks and clumps of grass to their satisfaction, and watching the sun begin to dip, casting long shadows across the landscape, they started their descent. Finding a large, relatively flat area, Tamsin whisked the frisbee out of her pocket and held it up. She had all her dogs' attention instantly, though Scruff, now being led by Emerald, was still clueless.

Tamsin named each dog by turns as she floated the frisbee away. "Don't want any mid-air collisions," she explained to Emerald. Then after a few throws she suddenly screeched "*MOONBEAM!!*" as the wind caught the toy and sent it precariously near the fenced edge of a quarry. Moonbeam stopped in her tracks, looking puzzled. She'd had her eyes fixed on the frisbee and was unaware of the danger she'd been in. Banjo ran and retrieved the toy which had curved back round and landed in safety amongst the gorse bushes, and delivered it to Tamsin.

"Enough of that," she said, patting her heart with her hand. "I'll stick to safer places for this game in future!" and she shoved the toy into her back pocket again, the dogs looking slightly crestfallen.

"They love it - and I'm amazed how you managed to stop Moonbeam there. I had no idea they were so obedient."

"You just see them loafing about at home and performing the odd trick for fun. But an instant stop is one of the first things I teach them - that's why they're able to have such freedom on walks, because I know they'll respond."

"It's about trust, rather than control," observed Emerald thoughtfully.

"It is," and Tamsin smiled fondly at her crew, now trotting along around her, ready to get home for their dinner.

CHAPTER TWENTY-SEVEN

There was an urgent text from Feargal on Saturday morning, asking for a meet-up. Tamsin picked it up after leaving her first home visit - with an eight-week-old West Highland White puppy called Angus, as cute as a button.

I'll be in CS at 1230 - will that do? she tapped back hastily, before setting off to her next session, with someone who wanted their dog to become their assistance dog.

The phone beeped just as she was about to engage first gear. *A-ok!* she read. Really, it was like being in a gangster movie. Still, Feargal was certainly proving very useful with the information he was able to extract from people.

When she arrived at The Cake Stop, she went straight to the counter to get coffee. And *no* cake. Jean-Philippe greeted her with enthusiasm with a loud *"Bonjour Madame!"* and nodded to a table up at the end of the cafe half hidden behind a pillar, where she could see Feargal poking away at his laptop with two fingers.

"Why don't you learn to type properly?" she asked as she sat down opposite him. "It would save you hours."

"You're right. But I never seem to have the time to book onto a course."

"You don't need a course! My mother ensured I could type fast before I was twelve, by the simple expedient of ruling that to earn thirty minutes time playing computer games we had to do ten minutes of the touch-typing program."

"Not a bad idea."

"Early example of the way rewards work. And if you break down a difficult task it's much easier to make inroads into it. That's what I've always found. And it's why I can type so fast - thanks Mum!" She took a welcome sip of her coffee.

"You're right, I'll give it a go. You make it sound easy. Want to hear the latest?"

"A-ok!" she laughed.

Feargal looked slightly abashed, then said, "They've matched a fingerprint on the stick in the woods with some partials found at Phil's cottage. We need to visit Susan again - and talk to her niece!"

"How did you arrive at that idea? It's just what Emerald and I were working out only yesterday."

"Great minds! She's got to be involved. I don't believe in coincidences. And her and this Gary bloke - who must be of a similar age - both teenagers hanging around at the same time?"

"And how do you connect her to Gary?"

"Ah, well, I ran into your friend Charity yesterday. Mine of information she is! And she seemed to think there may be something there."

"Got it. Yes, that's what we were thinking. We tried all sorts of ideas, but couldn't make much sense of any of them. You doing any better?"

"Yup." He looked like the cat who'd got the cream. "This guy at Shirley's place - you're dead right. He's her son. *And* he did seven years for robbery. Must have been viewed very seriously to get that long. That's when Shirley moved here, when he got locked up. She was in the centre of Birmingham and she wanted a safer place for her son once he was out. Not to mention get away from the stares and pointing fingers where she lived."

"Well, well, well."

"Three holes in the ground," quipped Feargal with a grin.

"What's his name?"

"It's Mark. Mark Bendicks. That's Shirley's married name, though she goes by Vaughan here, as you know."

"You know what, maybe that's a possible blackmail I didn't think of - that Phil had found out about Mark and was blackmailing Shirley. And now Mark's arrived here, perhaps she didn't trust Phil to keep his side of the nasty bargain."

"That's a definite maybe for me."

"And I wonder where the connection with Gary came from?"

"Motor bikes?" suggested Feargal. "They both have bikes."

"Ahh, that figures. They could enjoy racing, or doing them up, or whatever it is bikers like to do. Perhaps prison had workshops on motorbike maintenance, so their customers have a skill when they emerge. Maybe their meetings here were entirely innocent. Well, innocent as far as we're concerned. Who knows whether Mark is rehabilitated - reformed - whatever they call it."

"I'm going to do a bit of sniffing about. There's a motorbike shop in the Link," he said, referring to yet another of the many Malverns. "Seems to be a place where they hang out and chat while they buy bits and bobs for their bikes and get oil all over themselves."

"You'd better look a bit more biker-y when you visit! Got a leather jacket, or some black boots?"

"I'll find something, don't worry. Always prepared, me," he smiled. "Will we have a go at Susan now?" Feargal took the last morsel of his toasted sandwich and swiped his hands together to shake off the crumbs.

"I'm game! I'm free this afternoon - let's do it."

As they left, giving Jean-Philippe and Kylie a friendly wave, Tamsin was careful to go the long way round the magazine racks in front of the counter to avoid being confronted by the cakes again, as her stomach rumbled with complaint.

It was Sally who opened the door to them twenty minutes later. "I wondered how Susan was," said Tamsin. "I'd love to talk to her - her accident happened on my dog walk: I feel responsible!"

Sally looked unimpressed, but opened the door to usher her in. "This is my friend Feargal," Tamsin tossed over her shoulder as she passed Sally, "you don't mind, do you?"

Sally looked as though she did mind, but hearing Susan's quavering call of "Who is it?" from the sitting room she thought better of shooing them out again.

"Susan!" Tamsin rushed over, patting Frankie on the way. "How are you? I'm so sorry for what happened! Awful business! Whoever could have wanted to hurt you?"

Susan sat up a little from her reclining position on the couch, and shook her head sadly, winced, then kept it still again. "I really don't know. I just can't remember it at all clearly. I don't even know why I was in that wood!"

"How very upsetting for you. But you're on the mend now?" Tamsin nodded to the shaven patch on her head and the large hospital sticking plaster over it.

"Yes, I'm so glad to be home. Things are slowly coming back to me. Such a blessing that Sally was here to look after Frankie - and me," she smiled at her niece. "How did Frankie get here?" she said suddenly. "You weren't there, were you, Sally?"

"I brought him home with me," said Tamsin, noticing the quick shake of the head and strained smile on Sally's face. "Sally was worried about him and rang me, so I brought him round. I had no idea there was someone here."

"So, now you're beginning to remember things, can you think who might have done this?" asked Feargal quietly. "It seems it was no accident."

"The only thing I can think is that someone mistook me for someone else. All this violence suddenly - oh dear, what is the world coming to? They say that Malvern's one of the safest places in the country to live. But we've had two violent crimes within a few days of each other." Her frown deepened in her pale, grey face.

"It's worrying alright," said Tamsin. "Hey - are you able to put some of your amazing remedies on your head to make it better?"

"They won't let me. Say I mustn't remove the bandage till the next check-up. I certainly will once I can get to it. I've got Arnica in the cold greenhouse, and Aloe Vera on the kitchen windowsill - they'll both help."

"You have an amazing gift with plants," said Tamsin, reflecting that if Phil had been poisoned this case would have been a lot easier to solve.

"Learnt at my mother's knee," she smiled.

"What about you Sally," asked Feargal, "did you learn it all too?"

"Only a little," Sally broke her silence. "I'm not green-fingered, I'm afraid."

"Susan, the police have been grilling me - I'm sure they asked you loads of questions too - and it's really awful for my business! So if you can think of anything at all that may help us find who did this, do let me know, won't you?"

"Alright dear," Susan sounded friendlier than she ever had before. "I appreciate your concern."

"Will you be able to come to class on Monday?"

"I'm hoping so. I have the check-up on Monday morning. I should be able to drive there. And if I can't drive but feel well enough for class, Sally can bring me."

"Excellent!" Tamsin stood up.

"I'm afraid I haven't done any practice with Frankie," Susan added apologetically.

"Don't worry! We'll catch you up. He's a lovely dog ... he enjoyed his brief stay at my home, too." She forebore to mention that he appeared totally unmoved by what had happened to his owner. "But he was really pleased to get back here!" she added, hoping to soothe Susan.

As they were shown out of the house, Feargal pointed amongst some bushes lining the path and exclaimed, "What's that?"

Sally came out to look. "I can't see anything," she said.

"Oh, it was just some big beetle, I think," laughed Feargal, having got her outside the house as he wanted. "Tell me Sally, were you at the walk? You didn't say ..."

"Of course not," she blustered. "What would I be doing on a *dog* walk?"

"Just wondered." He changed to a different tack, "I suppose Phil's place is quite near here, isn't it? Nether Trotley seems to be a small village."

Sally narrowed her eyes, "The murdered man? He lived over that way," she waved her hand towards some distant trees. "Why do you ask?"

"Just curious!" Feargal reached out to shake her hand and gave a little bow. Tamsin reckoned this was one bird he wouldn't be charming out of a tree any time soon.

CHAPTER TWENTY-EIGHT

Tamsin had spent the weekend not thinking about the murder. Well, she tried, but with a varying amount of success. She really needed to give her brain a break and allow all the information swirling about there to settle, and for things to become clearer.

There was something nagging at her. Something she'd seen or heard that didn't ring true ... amongst all the other things she'd seen and heard that were clearly not true! Lies and prevarications, avoidance and denial. People were very good at deluding themselves, she reflected, and smiled at her dozing dogs. They were sleeping off their latest walk and waiting patiently for dinner time.

"Dogs are no trouble!" she declared to them. Moonbeam, who had been curled up under Quiz's chin, looked up hopefully, while Banjo flicked one of his pointy ears in Tamsin's direction. Scruff stayed dozing in the corner.

"You're just so uncomplicated," she sighed.

"Talking to yourself?" asked Emerald as she joined her in the living room.

"Yeah. Taking a break from thinking too hard!"

Emerald surveyed the furry heaps around the room, and smiled at

Opal who was curled up in the middle of the enormous and expensive fluffy dogbed. "How was your walk? They look flat out!"

"We had great fun with their frisbee-catching today. They're getting really good at it. Well," she added, "they've always been good at it. It's me who's getting better at throwing the thing!"

"That wrist-flick trick working?"

"It is! And as long as it's not too windy, I can steer it much better. And no more frisbee-throwing beside a sheer drop for us! That nearly gave me a heart attack the other day. The Common's perfect for it. The Nature Reserve will work well too .. and those Downs you were pointing out the other day."

"You and your Dog Walk Map!"

"Talking of dog walks, I had an idea. Just for fun, that's all."

"Oh yeah?"

"Yes. I thought I'd offer a special dog walk to the Trotley class on Tuesday, to make up for all they've been through."

"But one of them's a murderer!"

"*Maybe* one of them's a murderer. But that means there are at least four who are not."

"You know who'll want to be there to watch them all?"

"Hawkins?"

"No, silly! Feargal!"

"Now that's an idea ... I'll let him know when I've fixed the time. Good idea!"

And so at the class on Monday evening, Tamsin floated her idea. First of all she reminded them what fun the walk had been - right up till the drama with Susan - and they were enthusiastic at the prospect of another.

"I loved it!" called out Cameron.

"So did I!" added Alex, jumping out of his seat.

"And I'd like Mummy and Amanda to come too," said the youngest, Joe.

"So they shall, Joe - what a thoughtful boy you are," said Tamsin quietly to the little boy, and Charity nodded and leant over and patted him on the head.

"Great! That's fixed then," said Tamsin, when everyone had agreed. "We'll meet at the Common car park tomorrow at 6. And this time we'll all keep together and in the open."

"I won't be able to walk far, not with my leg," Jean wanted to be sure they'd all heard her saying that amidst all the chatter. "But Mr.Twinkle-toes loved all the attention - didn't you, darling? - so I wouldn't want to miss it."

"We'll make sure you can enjoy it too, don't you worry!" and Tamsin moved into the lesson.

Apart from Susan, surprisingly everyone had done some homework, and the boys were particularly keen to show off Buster's latest trick.

"I call him, you see," explained Cameron carefully, "and I stand like this." He demonstrated standing with his back turned and his feet far apart. "And he comes racing in and stops right between my legs."

"That sounds cool!" Charity coo-ed, speaking in what she called 'young-person-speak'.

"It is!" chorused Alex and Joe. "Just you see!" said Alex, proud of his big brother.

And sure enough, Alex held Buster's lead while Cameron ran down the hall and stopped with his back to them all - calling Buster loudly with huge excitement, flapping his arms.

Buster surged forward, Alex dropped the lead, and Buster hurtled in between Cameron's legs and screeched to a halt, eagerly awaiting his treat.

The rest of the class all clapped and applauded the little boy's trick with his dog.

"Ahh, that's lovely," said Susan, while the normally-surly Shirley smiled and nodded.

Jean turned to her little dog and said, "Don't go getting any ideas Twinks! You'd have me over if you did that!"

Chas beamed with pride at his boy. Tamsin was very impressed with his dedication - she knew it took time to teach a dog a trick - and told him so. And she gave him a prize of a tug toy, which he received with shining eyes.

After seeing what the little lad could do, everyone was inspired to achieve something with their own dog, and the rest of the class went swimmingly. There seemed to be a camaraderie between these students. Surely one of them … Tamsin shoved the thought from her mind as she helped Jean and her tiny dog negotiate some walking without either of them tripping up the other. This meant that Mr.Twinkletoes had to be quite far out from Jean's side to avoid getting trodden on or clouted with her stick.

Something pinged in her mind … no, it was gone again.

Shirley needed some help getting her big dog to sit evenly without his back legs splaying out around him. And Tamsin left her working on using her treat to get Luke to change his posture to a healthier position.

Charity was working on teaching Muffin not to snatch the toy or the treat from her hand. "Oh, that's so much better! That's polite, Muffy-muffs," she said, as the little dog understood that she needed to wait a moment and she'd still get her prize.

They left in high spirits, Chas escorting everyone out to their cars as he had the week before amidst cheery goodbyes, and Charity keeping Tamsin and Banjo company till they were all packed up and ready to go.

"The Furies were asking after you," said Charity as she swept the floor. "They so enjoyed your event. They may seem like three typical spinsters, but they do love to see the children having such a wonderful time."

"There's nothing 'typical' about those three indomitable sisters!" retorted Tamsin, packing her box. "I was showing them the photos in the Mercury when I dropped round on Friday to settle up. We do have some quirky folk in Malvern," she added, turning and raising an eyebrow in Charity's direction.

"Well, this quirky person wonders if you have an ulterior motive in arranging this walk tomorrow …"

"There are no flies on you, Miss Cleveland," she smiled. "I'm sure we're missing something really obvious - I've just got that feeling. And maybe with everyone relaxed together, something will just pop up. Someone will remember something, notice something, realise something they saw was significant. There's a clue lurking in the back of my mind and I just can't grab it ..."

She stacked the last two chairs before hefting the box onto her hip and calling Banjo. "I dunno. Somebody - apart from the obvious one - has to know something. Maybe this will jog their memory?"

CHAPTER TWENTY-NINE

Feargal was keen to join the walk. "I just want to see this crowd together on their own. Want to see how they are with each other," his voice emerged from the phone on the kitchen table.

"Same here," agreed Tamsin. "I just have the feeling ... something's got to give."

"Are you bringing our chief witness today?"

"No, I'm not. He's really upset when he sees any of them. It was an awful experience for him. So I don't think he'll point the paw."

"A dog walk with no dogs??" laughed Feargal.

"I'll bring my own three. They'll bulk out the numbers and give a good example." She paused, looking at her dogs - one asleep, one with half an eye on her and the third bristling with energy, ready to leap into action - then added with a grin, "I hope! Banjo will just keep himself to himself. The others will join in."

So Tamsin arrived early at the car park and spent a while taking the enthusiastic edge off her dogs by practising their frisbee-catching again. Banjo was the most agile of her dogs, and would make astonishing leaps to snatch the disc out of the air. After one spectacular catch she heard a smattering of applause, and turned to see some of her people had arrived.

"Can we teach Buster that?" asked Alex, bouncing on the spot in his excitement.

"I'd love that," added Cameron with a dreamy look in his eye.

"Yeah, can we?" As ever, Joe was not to be left out.

Chas stood behind his three boys, one hand on Joe's shoulder and one on Buster's lead. Just joining him was Molly with Amanda in her pushchair saying "Mm-mmm-mmm," and waving her hand vigorously to show off her biscuit.

"Sure, I can teach you that. But you'll have to be patient. You start with Buster catching it right in front of you - it takes time to get to the exciting part. Do you think you can do that," she addressed Cameron. He was the oldest, but also the most sensible - and dead keen.

Cameron nodded with enthusiasm. "Yes, I promise!"

"And you always have to make sure you're in a safe place so Buster can't injure himself," she added, guiltily.

The slow scrunching of tyres on gravel had them all turning to see Susan arriving with Frankie, and - surprisingly - Sally. They got themselves organised and joined Chas's family group.

Next to arrive was Charity with Muffin. She jumped out of the car with an alacrity that belied her grey hair, and came forward to chat with the children.

Shirley arrived with Luke. She had her young man in tow again - her son, as Tamsin now knew. She wondered why. Perhaps Shirley was nervous around these people. Or perhaps Mark knew something?

A very noisy gravel-crunching announced the arrival of Jean's car. They all looked in surprise at this dramatic entrance, then saw Jean emerge from the passenger side - slowly and awkwardly - leaning heavily on her stick, with her little dog hopping about beside her, one paw raised. "See you later then - don't be too long," she said as she closed her door. And the car accelerated loudly and shot off again with a lot more gravel-scrunching.

"Young men and cars!" she smiled indulgently, as she watched her vehicle now racing away. "Gary has some errands to run in town. He'll collect me later. Half an hour, didn't you say?"

"Probably longer than that - but he's welcome to join us, Jean. And we won't be far away as you don't want to walk too far. We'll be mostly in this area," Tamsin waved her arm to show the large grassy plain where they could walk easily as a group.

And so they set off on their walk. Tamsin's dogs were already calm, and she told each student when they could let their dog off the lead till gradually all the dogs would be loose.

Frankie loved his freedom and plunged about madly and clumsily. A stare from Quiz slowed him down and ensured he didn't crash into Tamsin and Banjo. Quiz knew that Banjo didn't like dogs in his face, so she was always ready to stare them down before they reached him. So Frankie turned his attention to the other dogs.

Jean uttered a squeak of fear as he raced towards her tiny Chihuahua. But, as Tamsin had expected from this kind dog, he skidded to a halt and lay down on his tummy to get down to the little dog's level. A mutual nose-sniff later, and the two of them started a game, which consisted of Mr.Twinkletoes racing round and round the prancing Frankie, then diving under him between his legs just as he seemed about to be caught up.

This spectacle was hugely entertaining, and the children were shouting with laughter. Baby Amanda pointed with her fat little fingers and giggled. When it came to Buster's turn to be unleashed he took a shine to Moonbeam, and they scampered about together in boisterous terrier fashion, causing more squeaks of delight from the children.

"I don't think Luke should run around like that," said Shirley dubiously. "He's so big, he might hurt someone."

"Let me introduce him to Quiz," Tamsin called her biggest dog over. "She'll be fine with him, and she won't put up with any rough stuff."

After a pleasant enough greeting between the dogs, Shirley felt confident enough to release him, and was pleased to see him trotting quietly about with Quiz, happy to follow her and ignore the mayhem from the other dogs.

Tamsin smiled at Mark and reached forward, hand outstretched. "I saw you that day at your home. I'm Tamsin."

"Mark," he said gruffly, briefly shaking her hand. Shirley looked relieved and focussed on Luke's progress again.

"This is such fun," said Charity, her face shining as she watched Muffin join in with Moonbeam and Buster for a while, before deciding that sniffing the ground was more rewarding than all this running about.

Feargal was walking slowly beside Jean, who made rather a big deal of walking with great reliance on her stick. Something pinged in Tamsin's mind again, just as Buster careered into her legs, earning a glare from Banjo - ah no! - It was gone again.

So Tamsin fell into step with Molly, and helped her negotiate the pushchair round a clump of bracken. "I'll be glad when this one's walking," laughed Molly, as the pushchair lurched, one wheel dipping into a rabbit-hole.

"She has a splendid head of red hair! Just like her Dad's. Does she enjoy her position as the only girl in the family?"

"She sure does! Spoilt rotten. And I was glad to get some female support, I can tell you! I felt quite outnumbered till she arrived." She paused to check the ground in front of her. "Even Buster's a boy!"

"They're doing really well with him. Especially Cameron. I trust they help take care of Buster?"

"They all have their duties, which switch round each week so they can't argue. But they're boys, so they'll always find something to argue about," she smiled again.

"Feeding him?" asked Tamsin.

"Yes, there's feeding, bed-cleaning, and brushing. They each get a turn."

"Great idea! They're learning responsibility. You manage it all so well, I have to say, Molly."

The pushchair jolted and Amanda dropped her biscuit. She started to make yearning baby noises, pointing urgently at it. She struggled with her harness, desperate to reclaim her prize.

Into Tamsin's mind leapt a memory - a scene from long ago. She'd driven a friend to hospital when her little boy had fallen and injured his leg. They were given a wheelchair to transport him to the x-ray department, as he was quite unable to put weight on his sore leg. But as they passed the little hospital shop and the child's mother offered him an ice cream to cheer him up, he leapt from the wheelchair and trotted happily to the counter to choose one. "Needs must when the devil drives," the wise lady in the shop had said, as child plus ice cream were stowed safely in the wheelchair once more, his mother shaking her head in perplexity.

Molly picked up the remains of the biscuit and tossed it to Buster, who'd spotted his opportunity, and refuelled Amanda with a clean one, explaining that eating food from the floor was not done. Tamsin stared at the scene in puzzlement, wondering what was trying to fight its way out of her mind.

Chas was chatting to Sally, who appeared a little less frosty today. And Susan was looking so much better than she had even the day before. 'Is her greyness beginning to fade?' wondered Tamsin as she strolled over to join her.

"You're looking so much better, Susan."

"I'm feeling it!" she replied with a spark Tamsin had not seen before. "I'm so enjoying seeing Frankie having fun. We're normally on our own all the time, you see."

"He's certainly enjoying Mr.Twinkletoes. I don't think he's left his side the whole walk!"

"It's charming, isn't it. He's really a very gentle dog at heart. Just bouncy."

"Are you glad you came to the classes?"

"I am! He's got so much easier to manage. And this is fun!"

Tamsin thought, as she so often did, that it was amazing what a dog and a bit of fresh air could do for someone's world-view. Despite the recent dramas, Susan looked as though she was rejoining the land of the living.

Just then, a screech of tyres announced Gary's arrival back in the car park. Jean looked up keenly, then her shoulders slumped a little as she saw smoke emerging from the window as Gary settled down for a cigarette rather than joining her.

Feargal wandered over to Tamsin. "Not learning much, I'm afraid," he said quietly. "Susan looks happy enough, not guilt-ridden. Shirley is more concerned about protecting her son than anything else. Chas has a delightful happy family. Charity is being Charity. And Jean is struggling to put one foot in front of the other ..."

"There! That's it!" whispered Tamsin urgently. "That's what I've been trying to remember ..." She turned to stare at her friend, "Feargal, I've got it!"

CHAPTER THIRTY

"You know, don't you," Feargal said as he stood close in front of Tamsin, looking intently at her face.

"Let me think a minute .." She held her hand up and stepped back, turned to look at the clump of trees where Susan had been attacked, turned back again to look at Cameron and his brothers. "I have to think .." She shook her head slowly before taking another look at Gary, now standing near his mother, her eyes narrowing.

"Are you alright?" asked Susan, stepping forward, a concerned look on her face for her new champion.

Tamsin turned to her, a distracted look in her eye. "Thank you Susan, I think I'm fine. It's all going to be fine now."

"She knows what happened." Feargal said flatly.

"No!" said Susan and Sally together. Shirley took a step back and reached impulsively for Mark's arm.

Charity came nearer to Tamsin, looking into her eyes. "Do you want to tell us, dear?"

"Yes! Tell us!" shouted out Alex excitedly, before being restrained by his mother with a harsh hiss.

"Is it a story?" asked Joe, sitting cross-legged on the grass in readiness.

"Yes, Joe, it *is* a story. A very sad and bad story, I'm afraid," Tamsin began. "And I think you all deserve to know the truth. We've all been under a cloud of suspicion since that awful night. Every one of us, including me. And nearly everyone here is totally innocent, and should have that burden removed from their shoulders."

"You're so right," said Shirley, "it's been an awful two weeks."

"You're telling me!" said Chas, "I'll be glad to be in the clear."

"And this awful person should be dealt with!" Jean's voice rang out.

"And they will be, rest assured. It's like this," Tamsin began. "Phil was a strange person. Lonely, not trusting others, apart from his little dog who he did truly love. He was always a bit of an outcast. From his difficult childhood that marked him out as a bit weird and different, to the only way he felt he could count, in people's eyes - his habit of digging out people's secrets."

"And then blackmailing them." Feargal folded his arms across his chest.

"Yes. Blackmail is ugly."

Alex jumped up impulsively, "What's blackmail?"

"It's like if you said to Joe, 'I won't tell on you if you give me your sweets'," Chas explained, drawing his sensitive son closer to him, "It's a kind of bullying." Alex nodded sadly, and those watching guessed that he'd suffered for his jerky and spontaneous antics.

Tamsin continued, "And Phil was blackmailing quite a few people. Those he thought had a bit of cash to spare. He knew you had little money, Susan, so he just threatened you in return for free medication."

Susan opened her mouth as if to speak, was nudged fiercely in the ribs by Sally, and shut it again. She nodded silently, blushing hotly.

"Don't worry, we don't have to know what he had against you. That's gone with him," she added. "And Chas treated him with the contempt he deserved when he tried it on with him. Why, you've only got to take one look at Amanda to know that she's his!"

Chas gave a crooked smile and looked dotingly at his little daughter, now fast asleep in her buggy.

"Shirley .."

"No!" interrupted Shirley, "don't! Please."

Tamsin held up a calming hand. "Shirley had a small secret from way back that she wasn't anxious for anyone to know about. I guess Phil was working on the hedge near an open window when he overheard something he thought he could turn to his advantage. Let's just leave it at that, Shirley. But it explains the mystery of the break-in at Phil's cottage."

"Really?" asked Charity, open-mouthed, "How?" She looked about her urgently, as if the perpetrator would put their hand up.

"Mark. You resented this man extorting money from your mother - quite rightly. And at the motorbike shop you met someone else with a grudge against Phil, from having run into trouble with him way back, as a boy. That would be you, Gary, right?"

Mark and Gary both shifted uneasily. Mark moved closer to Shirley, while Gary started to look about him furtively.

"It was easy enough for you both to hatch a plan to recover some of this blackmail money, by breaking into the dead man's home and snooping about."

"But unfortunately for you, you were seen," added Feargal.

"By us," said Tamsin.

"You didn't see *me*," growled Mark.

"No, you must have already made a run for it, possibly with the money. It was Gary we saw. You were wearing that same hoodie that you're wearing now, Gary."

Gary looked about to escape, but as he stepped forward Jean put her stick across his chest. "You're not going anywhere, my boy," she said sternly.

"Reclaiming what had been stolen - that's not a crime!" Mark spoke out, Shirley clutching his sleeve.

"That's debatable," Tamsin looked at him with some compassion, "but it does explain that mystery."

"That doesn't get us any nearer who killed Phil," Susan spoke out. "Nor who attacked me! Have you thought of that?"

"The person who attacked you was trying to divert attention from the real killer. Gary knew about Phil's hold over his mother, and how it had broken her heart."

Molly looked aghast at Jean, "What hold, Jean?"

Jean scowled and kept her mouth firmly shut.

"So Gary guessed that his mother was somehow involved in this. On the day of the dog walk he knew she was staying back near the car park, with loads of witnesses, so - unbeknown to her - he approached the Common from the other end, saw his chance when Susan wandered into the woods to answer a call of nature," Susan blushed beetroot, "and whacked her with the nearest handy branch. It didn't matter who it was he hit, as long as his mother was far away at the time."

"You can't prove any of this!" snarled Gary.

"I think you'll find that the fingerprints the police found on the branch will match those found at Phil's cottage," said Feargal.

"As well as the ones on your hands!" Susan was regaining her composure.

"I thought you were wearing gloves?" said Mark.

"Shut up, you idiot!" barked Gary.

"Case closed, I'd say," Feargal grinned at Tamsin, who was in full flow now as everything was just clicking into place.

"You see, Phil had found evidence of crooked shenanigans at the Gardening Society Jean was a big noise in. Evidence of corruption in the judging. Possibly evidence of why Jean won so often ... And while his own morals were pretty poor, he felt strongly that she shouldn't continue in a position of power in the village. So he ensured that she stepped down from her previous duties of organising the shows and competitions. Whether he had also exacted money I don't know. But he was able at any time to turn the screw and compound his blackmail." Tamsin shifted position and turned towards Jean, whose lips were now a thin line.

"We know the order people left the car park after the class. Susan went first, followed closely by Shirley. Chas took a bit longer getting his flock safely into the car, while Jean made a big show of getting her dog's legs tangled in his harness. Once Chas was gone, with Charity and me inside the hall, that left her alone with Phil, who was still near his car."

Jean, her face paling, glowered at Tamsin.

"You make a big show of needing your stick to support you - part of the fiction that that's why you had to stand down from your position at the Gardening Society, isn't that so, Jean? That your leg is too bad to allow you to continue. But sometimes you forget. Like when you use your stick as a pointer, or a tool to jab someone's foot, or to restrain Gary just now. You can actually get about quite easily without it. When we visited you at home, you walked to the door evenly then went back to fetch your stick before letting us in and limping back down to the living room. It's a nice stick by the way - hand-carved, I think? A big heavy handle, with lots of nooks and crannies on it."

Charity's mouth by now was forming a big round O.

"Phil turning up at the class that day, and you having to be polite to him, was simply the last straw, am I right Jean? This man you considered beneath you, who had wrecked your life - though in truth you'd wrecked it yourself by your own actions - was now behaving as an equal beside you. It was too much, and you determined to tell him so."

Jean detected a glimmer of sympathy and looked pleadingly at Tamsin, but didn't speak.

"Perhaps you wanted to tell him to leave the class, to avoid the danger of being further humiliated by him? Or perhaps you just wanted to give him a piece of your mind. And when he laughed at you and turned away, there - in the dark and lonely car park - you boiled over, lifted your stick and gave him a firm whack round the back of the head with the heavy handle."

There was a stunned silence from the group who were hanging on Tamsin's every word. Jean began to sob quietly.

"You weren't to know he had an old injury which caused a weakness in his skull. Maybe it was a hangover from when his father used to beat him, who knows. But your blow was enough to kill him. You must have got an awful shock when you heard the news the next day."

Jean nodded miserably.

"I bet you scrubbed your stick carefully, once you learnt the appalling truth."

Feargal stepped towards her, hand outstretched. "I think the police will want to go over this for DNA traces," he said, gently taking the stick from her, holding it carefully by the shaft.

Jean reached for her son and leant heavily on him.

"He was a horrible man," she said, turning back to face them all. "He deserved what he got!"

A gasp came from the group - it came out like a loud rush of air.

"I never meant to kill him. He'd just pushed me too far ..."

"If the court sees it as manslaughter you won't get too long, I expect." Feargal said reassuringly.

"And Mark and Gary will probably just get a smack on the hand for the cottage nonsense," Tamsin went on. "But you attacked someone violently and without provocation, Gary! That will mean trouble. Quite possibly you'll be thrown out of the Army as well?"

Gary, whose face had been getting redder, suddenly pushed his mother away from him, and while she stumbled and fell, he turned and ran.

Feargal shouted "Hoy! Stop there!" and started to race after him. Tamsin froze for a moment then snatched her frisbee out of her back pocket. "Dogs!" she cried as she focussed on the best throw of her life.

The frisbee flew up long and true and floated over Gary's head, three dogs in hot pursuit. Banjo quickly overtook Feargal and leapt up on Gary's back to vault over his head to catch his spinning toy. Gary gasped and threw his hands up in the air to steady himself and shouted out.

Buster - who had joined in the race for the fun of it - saw his moment and knew just what to do. He ran between Gary's legs as Moonbeam stepped in front of him to avoid being landed on by Banjo. Between the two terriers, they sent their quarry flying and he landed with a crash on the ground.

While Feargal snatched Buster's lead from Chas who had joined the chase, and knelt on the dazed soldier's back while he tied his hands together, Banjo trotted happily back to Tamsin with his frisbee.

"You *clever* dogs!" she exclaimed.

"Did you see? Did you see?" shouted Alex, bouncing with glee.

"Buster catched the bad man!" said Joe, grabbing his brother and jumping with him.

"Buster's clever too, and so are you for teaching him so well," said Tamsin, smiling fondly at Cameron.

Cameron blushed and said, "I'd love to teach Buster Banjo's trick!"

"We can do that, Cameron. But maybe keeping his feet on the ground for now!"

Charity and Susan were attending to Jean, who was sitting on the ground sobbing, having been helped up from her spreadeagled position. Sally remained where she had been standing - she really couldn't be bothered to be nice to Jean.

"Gary ..." wailed the old woman disconsolately. "Oh Gary, why?"

Chas was talking into his phone, beside the kneeling Feargal, and Gary, still flat on his face on the ground. Tamsin was relieved - for the first time in a while - that the police would soon be here.

And in a surprisingly short time she heard the welcome wail of sirens.

CHAPTER THIRTY-ONE

"Bee-baw, bee-baw!" chanted all three boys in unison.

"Ba-ba, ba-ba!" Amanda joined in, having been woken from her nap by her brothers' jubilant shouting.

It was the same two policemen who'd come out to the hall at Nether Trotley - what seemed an age ago now.

"Got some customers for us?" asked the senior of the pair.

"Yes. Gary over there attacked Susan in the woods. I'm surprised you hadn't already found that out via the fingerprints."

"We're not quite as barmy as you think we are!" said the second policeman. "We were already following young Mr.Waterloe here on account of the surge in break-ins in the area whenever he happens to have leave."

Jean gave another huge sob.

"You've just pipped us to the post," said Officer 1.

"There's this lady too," Tamsin indicated Jean, now looking quite broken. "She has information for you about the murder in the car park."

"Oh really? Now, that's very interesting indeed. Has she admitted to it?"

"She has," said Tamsin, while Sally and Shirley nodded vigorously. "And Mr.Bendicks here has something to tell you too. I imagine he'd like to square that up quickly, given ..."

"No!" interrupted Shirley. "Don't, please, Tamsin. I can drive Mark to the station for you, Sergeant. I expect your car will be full. And we can sort out a solicitor ... Oh Mark!" she shook her head hopelessly.

Mark said dejectedly, "I was a fool. I want to keep my record clean. I'm not going b-" His shoulders slumped and he took his mother's hand. "It's not going to happen again. Whatever you say, Officer."

The Constable set about calling for another car, while the Sergeant cautioned the three miscreants and put Gary into the back of the Panda as soon as it arrived.

"You stupid cow!" he shouted at Tamsin, as he was being shovelled in. "Why don't you stick to training dogs?"

"I'd love to do just that!" she laughed, dishing out yet more treats to the large group of eager dogs surrounding her.

Jean was given a seat in the back of the slightly more luxurious squad car and her stick was placed in an evidence bag.

Once more Tamsin had an extra dog to manage, as she reassured a weeping Jean and took Mr.Twinkletoes gently from her grip before closing the car door.

Meanwhile a white-faced Shirley loaded her sullen son into her own vehicle and set off between the two police cars.

The remaining students watched in awe as the procession left.

"That was extraordinary!" said Molly, her face full of admiration. "How did you work it all out, Tamsin?"

"And did you plan all that for today?" asked Sally, who had been rejoined by her aunt and Charity.

"No! Not at all! But can you imagine - I've been so preoccupied by all this that it only needed the last clue to appear and it all slid into place."

"What was the clue?" Cameron's eyes were shining as he looked up at her.

"Actually, it was Amanda who solved it."

The family all looked at each other in puzzlement.

"*A-man-da?*" the three boys said in disbelief and disappointment.

"Yes!" laughed Tamsin, feeling the relief flooding over her at last, now the police had taken over. "She dropped her biscuit, and was straining to get out of her pushchair to get it. It reminded me of once seeing someone leap from their wheelchair when they wanted something desperately. They were quite able to walk when they needed to."

"Then Jean thumped Gary on the chest with her stick!" said Susan.

"That was the very last piece of the puzzle. I'd seen before that she could manage perfectly well without it. But it was then that I realised just why she had built up this bad leg story."

"You should be on the telly!" cried Alex, still hopping and whirling with excitement.

"Are you a plain-clothes policeman?" asked Cameron.

"Are you a spy?" demanded Joe. "James Bond! Ah-ah-ah-ah .." And the three boys all started making machine gun noises, Molly attempting to hush them.

At that moment, Frankie - having had a long and boring rest since their walk - spotted his new friend and leapt forward, wrenching the lead from Susan's hand. He and Twinks started their capers again, bringing much-needed smiles to everyone's faces.

"What do you think, Susan?" asked Tamsin. "Fancy a visitor for a while? It may be a long while, of course ..."

"I think I do!" Susan smiled. "It's lovely to see Frankie enjoying himself so much, and Twinks seems to have found a friend."

"There'll be no-one in Baynton to look after him now." Tamsin handed Twinks' lead over to her. "So that's one down," she smiled. "Just one more to home ..." She saw everyone beginning to look at the ground, staying silent. "But don't worry! I have the perfect home in mind for Scruff. Now this has all been resolved - and they've told me Phil had no family left whatever - I'll be able to arrange that."

They heard a friendly "halloo" from the road, and Emerald, heading back down the hill from her class, trotted over to join them, her yoga bag slung over her shoulder. She smiled politely at the remaining students and spoke to Tamsin in a stage whisper: "You didn't get much of a turn-out then," she said sympathetically, looking at the small group. "I hope it wasn't too dull."

She looked quite baffled by the uncontrolled laughter that ensued from everyone, and went on, and on ...

CHAPTER THIRTY-TWO

The next morning the phone rang. Tamsin was going to let it go to messages and she'd deal with it later - but heard, "Good morning Miss Kernick, Chief Inspector Bob Hawkins here. Could you ..."

She snatched the phone, "Hello Chief Inspector!"

"Ah, Miss Kernick, er, good morning to you. I just wanted a quick word with you. It was very helpful of you to capture our murderer for us, but I do have to caution you that we strongly discourage the general public from "having a go". You're probably aware of the tragic results that can occur?"

"Thank you Mr.Hawkins. I suppose you're right, but I didn't know I was going to capture anyone till it all happened. But - you must be delighted at the clear-up of this puzzling crime?"

"Indeed. And, of course, we'd have got there ourselves soon enough," he blustered. "We already had Waterloe under obbo. We were on to him. The Army are very protective of their people, you know, so it was taking longer than we'd have liked to match the prints on the stick and at the scene of the break-in."

"Ah well, it's all sorted now. How long will they get?" Tamsin's curiosity got the better of her.

"It's hard to say. Mrs.Waterloe has mitigating circumstances, but I don't know how much she wants her involvement in the scam at the Gardening Society to be publicised. And it does seem to be medically proven that it was an accident."

"But she'll have to go to prison?"

"Probably a few years at least. She's not exactly a danger to the Community, unless you want to win the prize for the best Dahlias, that is ..."

Tamsin smiled - fancy the Inspector having a sense of humour!

"And her son - there's quite a few burglaries to lay at his door, along with GBH - er, that's Grievous Bodily Harm - not to mention anonymous phone calls."

"That was him too? He even made one to his own mother .."

"The Army probably won't want him back when he's served his sentence. Definitely a few years. So that dog of theirs will be needing a new home."

"Already sorted! And let's hope when they emerge they decide to start a new life somewhere else, like Mark Bendick's mother did."

"That's often encouraged."

"Well, nice to meet you, Mr.Hawkins, and I hope you don't take this the wrong way, but I hope we won't be meeting again!"

"If you can stop your students murdering each other, we'll be just fine."

She could hear the smile in his voice as he hung up.

Emerald floated down the stairs as she heard the call end. "YOU are coming to The Cake Stop this afternoon. I've been deputed to ensure you get there. And all the dogs are to come."

"Goodness! What's going on?"

"That would be telling. But you can come, can't you? I sneaked a look at your wall calendar and you seem to be clear this afternoon, right?"

"I am. And you know what? I think I deserve a massive slice of the Furies' best."

"Dog trainer turned detective! We can celebrate your new career."

"Oh no, I never want to have to go through all that again ... although, now you mention it ... it *was* fun, wasn't it?"

They laughed together as Emerald started juicing oranges and clattering coffee cups.

The dogs all looked interested at the prospect of comestibles. Quiz came over and pressed her big head against Tamsin's thigh, while Moonbeam and Scruff sat politely side by side, hoping to elicit a crumb or two.

"I suppose Scruff is going to stay now?" asked Emerald, deftly moving the milk carton away from Opal's curious paw.

"No," said Tamsin slowly, "I have a plan for him. In fact - what's the time? I think I just might catch her on her way back from the school run ..."

"Catch who?" asked Emerald to the closing door. "I'll hold off on the coffee then ..." she said to the empty space.

Tamsin walked fast to the Common. She reckoned she should be about in time to catch Val on her way home after delivering Jenny to school. And there she was, going up the hill! She had paused to pick a buttercup for her little boy, who was reaching out for it with both hands, like Amanda for her biscuit.

"Hi Val!" she called out, beginning to puff her way up the hill towards her, thinking, maybe more cake isn't such a good idea - perish the thought! I'll just have to walk the dogs more.

She drew Val slightly away from the pushchair so the little boy shouldn't overhear her suggestion. And with her back to the child, she said, "You know that man who died? The one with the little dog? Well, they've found out who did it and it's all dealt with now."

"That's a relief! Don't like to think of murderers wandering about free."

"So ... I still have his little dog, Scruff. The one Jenny fell for?"

Val nodded slowly, her eyes narrowing.

"Thing is, I know you said you'd find a puppy hard to manage, but Scruff is about three, and well housetrained. He's no trouble in the house. Settles happily to sleep most of the day. He's small, doesn't need a groomer, gentle, gets on well with other dogs. What I'm trying to say is .."

A smile was spreading over Val's face. "I think I know where this is going …"

"Well, if you'd like to have him, I'd be happy to give you a free class or two to get you started."

"Done!" Val's smile broadened. "To be honest the price of a dog - and classes - was something else that was holding me back, being on my own, you know. But this sounds perfect! Jenny will be absolutely thrilled!"

So they sealed the deal with an exchange of phone numbers, and they arranged a time for the handover.

"I've got a small dog bed he's been using while he's been with me. These things seem to accumulate down the years, you know! I'll bring it with me, and some of the food he's been having, to help him settle in."

As Tamsin strolled back to her house, she reflected on what a lot the Common had witnessed in the last couple of weeks. The ancient commonland had been there for so long, had seen so much .. and it never told.

CHAPTER THIRTY-THREE

"Come on slowcoach," called Emerald, throwing her bag over her shoulder, "You'll be late for The Cake Stop."

Tamsin clattered the keyboard of her laptop. "Sorry, just sending off a couple of emails. Enquiries are flowing in nicely after the big dog walk."

"Anybody after classes at Nether Trotley?" asked Emerald with a crooked grin.

"Believe it or not, yes! Both of those enquiries were for that area. Maybe murder's not such a bad career move after all," she quipped as she shut the laptop before it shut itself under the weight of Opal's chin resting on the top of it. "Coming .."

Emerald refused to answer any questions about Jean-Philippe's summons to the cafe as they walked happily through the pleasant sunny but cool day. They took a shortcut across the Common, then putting the three dogs back on lead, carried on to their rendezvous.

And as they came through The Cake Stop's big front door, a shout went up from the table in the window, followed by applause from Jean-Philippe and Kylie at the counter, laughter from Feargal and Charity, and looks varying from appreciation to extreme puzzlement on the faces of the other patrons.

Jean-Philippe came forward and gave Tamsin a hug, reaching down to pat Quiz on her big head, and nod to Banjo and Moonbeam. He knew better than to try to pet Banjo, and Moonbeam didn't need any encouragement to jump up.

"Welcome, great detective!" he declaimed, and a ripple of applause went through the cafe as people began to realise who Tamsin was.

"You will be giving *Hercule* and *Tintin* a run for their money, *non*?" he laughed.

"Oh, I don't know about that," Tamsin smiled as she manoeuvred her flock over to the window to settle them with the foodtoys she'd brought for them. "Hi Charity, Feargal!"

"We simply had to celebrate your success, my dear," said Charity, hanging on to Muffin who was anxious to greet her pals.

"So we've arranged a little something for you," continued Feargal.

"First of all, what would you like - your usual?" interrupted Jean-Philippe, then passed Tamsin and Emerald's order with a nod across to Kylie manning the machines.

"What's this 'little something'?" Tamsin turned to Feargal, with an anxious look on her face.

"Well, for a kick-off, you'll enjoy tomorrow's paper."

"Oh no! You haven't written about it all?" she wailed.

"Oh yes! I most certainly have. I am a news-hound, after all," he grinned, then waved his hands in a calm-down motion. "But hold your horses! You'll love it. Really. I've explained that the murder was down to an old feud in the area and nothing to do with you whatever. But that what you found out in an effort to clear your own name led the police to arresting the miscreants. Hawkins should be happy with that - leaves him in a good light."

"You're the heroine!" said Jean-Philippe.

"It should do wonders for your school now, Tamsin." Charity sat down and returned Muffin to her lap as she made space for Emerald to draw up a chair.

"And people have been talking about you already," said Kylie as she appeared with a tray of coffee mugs. "Whenever I hear them I tell them how brilliant you are!"

"All publicity is good publicity," murmured Emerald, reaching for her coffee.

"Or, as Oscar Wilde said, 'The only thing worse than being talked about is not being talked about'." Feargal smiled. "You'll find a renewed interest in dog training all of a sudden - specially when they read about Banjo's escapades with Buster and the frisbee."

Tamsin's mouth fell open. "Is there still time to stop this article?"

"No chance!" laughed Feargal, "Not without a court order - the Editor is loving it - and so should you!" He smiled at her, "and you don't want to put him off his latest idea!"

"What idea, Feargal?" asked Charity, Tamsin still being speechless.

"'Ask the Dog Trainer'! He's thinking of a monthly column."

"Wow! That would be amazing," Tamsin at last found her voice.

"Time to stand tall," said Emerald.

"And accept the compliments," added Charity.

"If people are interested in the frisbee thing, maybe I could run a Trick Dogs course ..." Tamsin's business hat returned to her head as she chewed this over.

"*Absolument!* That's more like it!"

"I ran into Shirley this morning," began Charity, which turned all eyes to her. "She explained about how she'd moved here to start a new life when her son had gone to prison. What a nice person he was underneath it all, you know the sort of thing mothers say. Anyhow she's got a solicitor onto it and hopes he'll only get a slap on the wrist for his part in the break-in, as he didn't actually take anything. She's determined to keep him well away from Gary and his ilk, and is looking to get him onto some training program for mechanics."

"Poor Shirley, she's been carrying a lot around on her shoulders. We'll have to make a special effort for her next Monday, Charity. It's probably good that it's out in the open now, no more awful secrets for her to hide."

At that moment the door burst open and in came a motley procession of sisters. Damaris, Penelope, and Electra Dodds bore a large tray covered with a cake box. They advanced on Tamsin's table and Electra made a space for the tray. Penelope lowered it to the table as Damaris lifted the cake cover with a flourish.

"Congratulations!" they chorused, as the others all echoed their "Congratulations!"

A splendid cake was revealed, with 'Tamsin the Malvern Hills Detective' written across the top, a little marzipan deerstalker and magnifying glass nestled in the thick icing, and a yellow frisbee leaning against the side of the cake.

Tamsin pressed her hands to her cheeks, as tears threatened to start. "Thank you! I don't know what to say ... but - thank you!"

Emerald leant across with her phone to snap a photo of the marvel.

"We're only glad you solved the mystery so quickly," boomed Penelope. "Jolly worthwhile person to have around, I say."

"We wanted you to know how pleased we are not to be looking over our shoulders every day," quavered Damaris.

"And this is how we can show you - compliments of Dodds & Co," added the floaty voice of Electra, as she took the pile of plates from the waiting Kylie, who had also brought a large knife for Damaris, already gleefully cutting the cake.

More chairs were brought to the table and coffees for the Furies, as the party began in earnest.

Amongst all the chatter, Tamsin took time to tell the sisters how grateful she was for their catering help on the big dog walk. "I call it the Big Dog Walk to differentiate it from the Momentous Dog Walk the following week! It's brought a good few new clients in," she went on enthusiastically. "So the sandwiches were a worthwhile investment. I'll be planning more of these walks - will you be able to supply the food again?"

"Certainly, m'dear," the loud voice of Penelope boomed out as Damaris drew breath and Electra looked other-worldly, as usual. "Happy to help you. Aren't we, gels?" The other sisters nodded dutifully as Electra added mysteriously, "We know we'll be getting to know you much better .. in the future."

Damaris picked up the knife and pointed to the cake, "Who'd like a little more?"

"Yes please," said Feargal eagerly, holding out his plate.

Tamsin looked at the stick-thin figure of the young man and sighed, holding a hand over her plate and giving a sad but polite "No thanks, Damaris".

Little did she know that the box that had covered the cake would be triumphantly carried home by Emerald later that day, and that she'd be eating cake for days!

TO FIND *out how Tamsin arrived in Malvern and began Top Dogs, you can read this free novella "Where it all began" at*

https://urlgeni.us/Lucyemblemcozy

and we'll be able to let you know when Tamsin's next adventure is ready for you!

If you enjoyed this book, I'd love it if you could whiz over to where you bought it and leave a brief review, so others may find it and enjoy it as well!

ABOUT THE AUTHOR

From an early age I loved animals. From doing "showjumping" in the back garden with Simon, the long-suffering family pet - many years before Dog Agility was invented - I worked in the creative arts till I came back to my first love and qualified as a dog trainer.

Working for years with thousands of dogs and their colourful owners - from every walk of life - I found that their fancies and foibles, their doings and their undoings, served to inspire this series of cozy mysteries.

While the varying characters weave their way through the books, some becoming established personnel in the stories, the stars of the show are the animals!

They don't have human powers. They don't need to. They have plenty of powers of their own, which need only patience and kindness to bring out and enjoy with them.

If you enjoyed this story, I would LOVE it if you could hop over to where you purchased your book and leave a brief review!

Lucy Emblem

facebook.com/lucyemblemcozies

Printed in Great Britain
by Amazon